S0-ANE-999

THE WEANING
and other stories

Also by Nell Brasher

Angel Tracks in the Cabbage Patch
Daddy Poured the Coffee
You've Got to be Kiddin'!
Queenstown Chronicle

THE WEANING
and other stories

Nell Brasher

CRANE HILL
PUBLISHERS
Birmingham, Alabama
1993

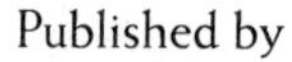

Published by

CRANE HILL
PUBLISHERS
2923 Crescent Avenue
Birmingham, Alabama 35209

Cover illustration by Dwayne Coleman

Library of Congress Cataloging-in-Publication Data

Brasher, Nell.
The weaning & other stories / by Nell Brasher. — 1st ed.
p. cm.
ISBN 1-881548-01-5 :$19.95
1. Country life—Alabama—Perry County—Fiction. 2. Family—Alabama—Perry County—Fiction. 3. Perry County (Ala.)—Fiction. I. Title. II. Title: Weaning and other stories.
PS3552.R3277W43 1993
813'.54_dc20 93-33458
CIP

Contents

Introduction

I had just finished reading Graham Greene's short story "Across the Bridge" to my fiction writing class, and after a few moments I invited the class to comment on the story.

"I don't know if I can like a story about a man who kicks his dog," came one voice. "That ruins it for me."

I looked at the speaker, a tiny, stern-eyed woman in a pertly curled brown wig. She said nothing of the story's structure, its theme, nor its masterful use of positioned observer point of view. All that mattered to Nell Brasher was that this character was not likable — not to her, anyway. A man who kicked his dog, for whatever reason, was unredeemable, so what good was the story?

I found her visceral, nonanalytic reaction to the story refreshing and asked her to elaborate. But no, that was all she had to say, and she wasn't about to critique the story on any level but the personal. As the term progressed, I expected her to produce moralistic stories that would summarily condemn dog-kickers, romanticize little girls who brought home stray rabbits and baby deer, and neatly divide all of humanity into the decent and the decadent.

Instead, I found in Brasher's writing an eye that at once views the human race with the impartiality of a stranger and the fondness of a friend. Brasher depicts her characters' failings not only as shortcomings but also as the very strengths that will allow them to survive their own lives. And for Brasher's people, life is a hazardous affair, a constantly unfolding bedlam that sucks them ever deeper into the vortex of a situation that starts out innocently but then gets out of hand. The narrative eye of Nell Brasher does not assign blame for the chaos these people deal themselves, nor does it celebrate their victories with bland piety or self-serving smugness. It simply chuckles, shakes its head, and moves on to the next curve in the road.

Nell Brasher, who died in 1992, was a master of short story structure, a traditionalist with an instinctive and unerring sense of beginning, middle, and end. A typical Brasher story opens on a character with a dilemma, builds inexorably to a climactic scene in which the world as these people know it is threatened with extinction, then winds down logically and yet, more often that not, unpredictably to an uneasy truce with the cosmos. It is this exquisite balance between the obvious and the surprising, the salient and the semisweet, that makes Nell Brasher a genuine artist of the short story.

Brasher's stories are, first of all, entertaining. She writes of the hard lives of country people in an era so recently passed that many can still recall it. In the hands of a lesser writer, these lives would have been as bitter and unforgiving as the hard clay land on which they were lived, but Brasher never allows her people to sink into the abyss of despair or to question their trials in the trivial, blame-placing ways that often characterize stories about ignorant, deprived people.

In this sense, Brasher writes in the Southern tradition of Erskine Caldwell and Flannery O'Connor, but with more stylistic grace than Caldwell, more warmth than O'Connor. Brasher clearly studied and drew from Caldwell's earthiness, and she has infused many of her stories with a brand of wicked, ironic humor that is reminiscent of O'Connor. But Brasher is less dark in her irony than either Caldwell or O'Connor, and she depicts disaster in a playful, at times even slapstick, way. Brasher's people personify maddening folly with the same nonchalance as they depict common sense and virtue. Some are considerably less virtuous than others: a self-important ne'er-do-well with pretensions to wisdom and a gentlemanly demeanor; a monstrous child of nearly three, whose mother wants only to graduate him from breast-feeding, but is reluctant to make the whole family pay the high price for this weaning; a family of poor people whose main source of food is church reunions and whose physical well-being depends on their quick-witted getaways.

Brasher's unfortunate lot was to have been a 1930s writer in the 1980s. Writing fifty years after her natural historical milieu and portraying the no-longer-fashionable rural life she knew so intimately, Brasher received scant attention. Her work was rarely published, and she lived the frustration of suspecting she was a far more talented writer than the world would ever know. A simple country woman, wife of a Baptist preacher, Nell Brasher lived a second dichotomy — that of the public churchwoman and private, secular writer, whose sense of humanity transcended the confines of dogma or ideology. Her stories are not dainty, her people are not righteous, her treatment of them is honest rather than earnest, and her conclusions, if there are any, are utterly nonjudgmental.

I invite you to sit for awhile at Nell Brasher's table. You'll find only the minimal utensils, and the servings will be sparse, but you'll come away from this simple, country supper with a feeling of having been not only fed—also nourished.

Fred Bonnie

The Weaning

Birdie and Eva Jane Alvester, two bony-legged girls, aged eleven and nine, scuttled along the dusty road like thistles before a wind, their loose cotton print dresses clinging to their sweating bodies. They passed Fosters' place and never slowed down until they approached Brodies'.

Only a narrow, freshly swept yard separated Brodies' front porch from the road. Virella Brodie sat on the porch shelling purple hull peas.

"Why, hello there chillern," she called out.

"Good morning, Mis' Brodie," Birdie said, slowing down.

"Stop and sit a mite," Virella invited. "I know you'uns are about tuckered out, walking in this heat, and all. Wet your gullets with a drink of water."

After a brief hesitation Birdie walked resolutely across the sandy yard, mounted the porch steps, and sat down in the swing.

"We got to hurry, Birdie," Eva Jane said, still in the road. "You said we got to hurry."

"You make my blood run cold, Eva Jane!" Birdie snapped. "It ain't no matter, us resting a mite!"

Eva Jane offered no more objections. She went over to smell one of the yellow roses on a bush by the steps.

"We're going to Burchfield's to get the b'nanners Mama sent for to wean Dolfus," Birdie said importantly.

"Yes," Virella said. "Well I declare I didn't realize the signs are right again, but I guess they are. I declare I hope she breaks him loose this time. Pore thing, she's plum wore out suckling that big young'un, and all. How old is he anyway?"

"He's two going on three," Birdie said. It made her mad and embarrassed her, too, for people to ask how old Dolfus was. He had already come out the victor in several attempted weanings. Now the signs were in the feet again, and Emma Kate, his mama, meant to give it another try.

Virella sighed. "Yes. Well, I declare I do believe yore Ma's too easygoing. He'uz mine, I'da already weaned him." Birdie jumped up. With scarcely a pause Virella asked, "Where's Ned? Why'nt he go to the store with you'uns?"

"Mama couldn't send him 'cause he'd eat up the nanners," Eva Jane answered.

Birdie was already in the road. "Come on here, Eva Jane," she ordered. "We got to hurry. You make my blood run cold fooling around talking!"

"I'm go tell Mama on you," Eva Jane said, trotting to keep up. "Her and Papa both told you not to say 'make my blood run cold' no more. Yore blood ain't cold nohow. You're just trying to copy Sweetie Foster."

Birdie rolled her eyes until only the whites showed. "I'm a good mind to put a hex on you, Eva Jane Alvester," she muttered.

"Stop that, Birdie," Eva Jane whimpered. "You're scaring me. Stop that scaring me!"

"Tattletale!" Birdie spat out. Then she began to run.

Reaching Burchfield's they went in to the big country store that smelled of onions, apples, leather, and kerosene. Mr. Burchfield greeted them. He was a short, quick-mannered little man with white whiskers and smiling blue eyes that darted all-seeing glances as he waited on customers.

"Hee," he chirped, twitching his shoulders and winking at them. "You all come to get the bananas, eh?"

"Yes, sir."

"Hee, third time your Ma's bought bananas to wean that chap. I hope she holds his feet to the fire this time."

Birdie stood with a stern, tight-lipped expression as Mr. Burchfield got the bananas from under the counter and noted the price of them on the debit side of Ruf Alvester's page in the charge book.

Eva Jane touched Birdie's elbow. "Can we charge a coker-colar, Birdie?" she asked.

"No! You know Papa says we ain't ever to charge no coker-colar!" But the desire for the Coke glittered in Birdie's eyes.

"Hee," Mr. Burchfield piped as he handed the brown paper sack to Birdie, "you chaps get yourself a drink and sometimes when your Pa gives you a nickel you can pay me. Man works at a sawmill after he lays his crop by oughta could afford to buy his young'uns a Coke. He oughta make good money riding that carriage. He still riding that carriage?"

"Yes, sir," Birdie replied as she popped the top off the Coke. She turned it up and let it gurgle. When it was empty, she made a smacking noise and belched loudly. Eva Jane took a little longer to swallow her Coke. Then they put down their empty bottles and left for home.

Walking fast, hardly speaking, they arrived home a little before noon. Birdie put the bananas behind the well curb, and then they crossed the hot sandy yard and slipped into the kitchen. Emma Kate was taking a pone of freshly baked cornbread out of the oven of the woodburning stove. Dolfus, in a knee-length shirt, had the cat by the tail, beating it, his laughter mingling oddly with the cat's meowing and spitting.

"Stop that, you cross-eyed baboon!" Birdie yelled, jerking Dolfus loose from the cat. "I'd like to beat yore tail. You make my blood run cold!"

Dolfus began to howl. Emma Kate picked him up, looking harried. "Birdie," she scolded, "Dolfus is not cross-eyed. I wisht you'd stop scaring him."

"You oughta beat him!"

"Papa told her not to say, 'blood run...'" Eva Jane began.

"Shut up!" Birdie's voice cracked like a whip. "Where's Ned?"

"I sent him to the lower garden atter some tomatoes," Emma Kate said. "Where's them b'nanners? Quick, before he gets back!"

Birdie sprang out the door and sprinted across the yard. In less than a minute she was back, and Emma Kate quickly hid the bananas in the meal box.

Ned, who was ten, came in with a pan full of red ripe tomatoes. "Where have you and Eva Jane been?" he demanded of Birdie.

"None of your business!" Birdie retorted.

"You better tell me!" He grabbed a tomato and drew back.

Birdie stuck out her tongue at him. He let go with the tomato, barely missing her head.

Emma Kate reached for her switch on the belting. "You young'uns stop that fussing!" she ordered, "Before I wear you out!"

"Where'd you go, where'd you go?" Ned began chanting in a singsong voice.

Emma Kate cut at him with her switch, but he bolted out the back door.

At that moment the noon whistle at Tompkins sawmill sounded a shrill blast. Ruf Alvester would be home for dinner in five minutes.

Emma Kate, a big lanky woman with her greasy black hair pinned in a knot at the back of her head, moved briskly about the hot kitchen, getting dinner on the table. For all her briskness she looked tired and drained out. Four children, hard work, and tight living had left her with only a trace of the strapping good looks she once possessed.

Ruf came in. Hanging his battered hat on a nail in the wall he washed his hands, dried them, and sat down to the table. Emma Kate brought a plate of sliced tomatoes to the table and sat down herself.

Dolfus whined to sit in her lap. She patted his chair. "Sit up here, Dolfus," she coaxed. "Be a big boy." He kept whining. She jumped him up into her lap.

"You got that chap spiled rotten, Emma Kate," Ruf said, without missing a bite of the fresh vegetables and fried chicken piled on his plate. A vein stood out in his bull neck. "That's the reason he's so dad-bogged much trouble to wean."

"Well, he's the baby, Ruf," Emma Kate simpered. Ruff didn't know about the bananas or the imminence of the weaning.

At the supper table that night Emma Kate announced the weaning.

"What about b'nanners?" Ruf asked. "You got any b'nanners?"

"I sent Birdie and Eva Jane to Burchfield's this morning atter them," Emma Kate said.

Popping up out of his chair Ned demanded a banana. Ruf jerked him back down.

"Leave them b'nanners alone, boy. Them b'nanners are gonna be used to wean Dolfus. I catch you atter one, I'll tan yore hide!"

Ned shoved his plate across the table and sprang to his feet screeching. Ruf grabbed for him but he got away.

At 7 p.m. Emma Kate began the blackening of both breasts. Ruf stood by to help.

"We've got to blacken 'em both pot black, Ruf. Get another swipe offen that stove lid and rub it on."

Ruf lifted a stove lid and raked the index finger of one work-roughened hand across the underside of the sooty lid. Then he went to rub more blackening around the nipples of his wife's breasts.

"Are you shore them signs are right, Emma Kate?" he asked.

"Certainly I'm shore! You think I'd wean this young'un if the signs wasn't right? You think I'm crazy?"

"Naw, Emma Kate, I don't think you're crazy. I jest wanted to know."

Dolfus, who had been beating the cat while preparations for the weaning were underway, now lost the cat and came to get in Emma Kate's lap. He went for his ninny. Confronted with the pot black nipple, he pulled back and began squalling.

"Ohm bite! Ohm bite!"

Emma Kate motioned for Birdie to hand her a banana. "Jest gimme half a one," she said.

Birdie leaped towards the meal box, took out a banana, broke it in two, and handed half of it to Emma Kate. She offered it to Dolfus.

"Looka heah," Emma Kate coaxed, "you don't want that old black titty, do you Dolfus? Let's throw it away and get a b'nanner. You want a nice ripe nanny-wanny, Dolfus?"

Dolfus knocked the banana out of Emma Kate's hand and kept squalling. "Ohm bite! Ohm bite!" It was plain to be seen that soon he'd take his ninny, soot or no soot.

"Hand me that bottle of turpentine offen the belting, Ruf, quick!" Emma Kate said.

Ruf handed her the bottle. Opening it she put a finger over the top of it and turned it upside down. She then dabbed both nipples with turpentine.

"First thing you know you'll be taking off like a turpentined dog, Emma Kate," Ruf warned. "That stuff will bodaciously burn you!"

"I ain't more'n teching it, Ruf. Anyhow, I got to wean this young'un, burn or not. I can't stand him pulling on me no longer. You don't know how it is having a young'un pulling on you like a yearling calf. Never knowing when he's gonna take a notion to bite me."

Pulling her dress so that her breast flipped back inside, Emma Kate again began wheedling Dolfus. "Hush, hush," she crooned. "Looka heah, where's the puppy? Heah, puppy, heah! Commere and get this old black titty. Dolfus don't want it. Heah, puppy, heah."

"We ain't got no puppy!" Ned hollered. "What'cha calling a puppy for? We ain't GOT NO PUPPY!"

Ruf swung at him with his open hand. Ned sprang out of his reach and made a dive for the meal box. "I'm onna have that other half of that b'nanner!" he shouted.

Birdie screamed. She landed on top of the meal box before Ned could lift the lid. Ruf bore down on him with a stick of stove wood. Circling, Ned stooped to snatch up the banana half that Dolfus had rejected and ran.

Dolfus was now kicking and squealing. Emma Kate raised a hand to signal for another piece of banana. She held it close enough for Dolfus to smell it. "Here, Dolfu," she cajoled, "you want some b'nanner? Dolfus likes nanny-wanny. Here, take a taste, Dolfus."

Dolfus stopped kicking and squealing, snatched the banana, gobbled it down, and resumed his noise. "Ohm bite! Ohm bite!"

At this point Emma Kate, with Dolfus in her arms, moved into the big unceilinged room that joined the kitchen. Ruf followed her. Ned came in the front door.

"I awnt a b'nanner," he said.

"You can't have a b'nanner, Ned," Emma Kate said. She sat down in one of the straight-backed chairs in the room and began bumping back and forth with Dolfus in her arms. "We ain't got but just enough b'nanners to wean Dolfus. Big boy like you oughta could understand that."

"He's already had half a b'nanner," Birdie sang out from the kitchen.

"I awnt a nanner!" he demanded.

"Hesh up, you sass-head!" Ruf shouted, heaving a mail-order catalog at Ned's head. Ned ducked and headed back to the kitchen. There he stepped up onto a chair and over onto the table where Birdie and Eva Jane were stacking dishes.

"I awnt a nanner, I awnt a nanner!" the boy screamed in a rising crescendo.

"Git offen this table, you devil!" Birdie yelled, grabbing at Ned's bony legs. "You make my blood run cold!"

Ned sprang to the other end of the table. A cup crashed to the floor.

"He broke a cup," Eva Jane wailed. "He broke the one with a handle on it!" She knelt down to pick up the pieces.

Ned kept chanting until he saw Ruf coming with a chair raised above his head, ready to throw it. Then he was gone again.

"I'm gonna bodaciously blister that chap I get my hands on him," Ruf growled, putting the chair down. He turned to Birdie, "I don't wanta hear no more of that 'blood run cold' out of you either, you hear me!"

"I ain't deef!" Birdie sassed.

Emma Kate put Dolfus down and began turning down the covers on one of the two beds in the room. Dolfus, still squalling, held onto the tail of his Mama's dress following every step she made.

"Won't nobody get no sleep here tonight," Ruf prophesied gloomily. "And I got to ride that carriage tomorrow. Got to be there ready to roll come six o'clock. Wouldn't surprise me if I fall in that saw and get cut to jiblets. Fellar can't work 'thout sleep."

Emma Kate sighed. Picking up Dolfus she sat down, put a hand into her low-necked dress, and brought out a breast. Dolfus lunged at it but as soon as he tasted the turpentine he let go and struck a new chord, with his head back like a dog baying at the moon.

Ruf pulled off his shoes and overalls. He crossed the room in his shirt tail and got into bed, pulling up some cover.

"I wisht you'd wait to wean that chap, Emma Kate," he said. "I got to get some sleep. You want me to get cut to jiblets?"

"I been waiting and waiting, Ruf. Every time I start to wean him you say, 'I wisht you'd wait.' If it was you he was pulling at you wouldn't be saying, 'I wisht you'd wait.'"

She put Dolfus on the bed with Ruf. He rolled over and got on his all fours, head down, back end up, howling steadily. All at once Ruf gave the elevated rear a resounding whack.

"Hesh that crying, young'un!" he bellowed. "You wanta suck till you're old enough to vote? I've got to get some sleep, you hear me!"

Dolfus made for Emma Kate. "You'll stunt his growth, Ruf, I do know!" she scolded.

At that moment a shriek split the air. It was Birdie. "Mama! Ned's trying to get them b'nanners." A sound of scuffling broke out in the kitchen.

With a roar Ruf sprang out of bed and headed for the kitchen, holding down his shirt tail with one hand, grabbing the broom with his other hand. Reaching the kitchen he turned his shirt tail loose and swung the broom handle, shattering the twenty-five watt bulb hanging from a rafter over the table just as Emma Kate turned off the forty watt bulb in the bedroom, plunging the house into darkness. Ned once more made his escape out the back door.

For a moment the unabated squalling of Dolfus seemed to fill the whole world. Then bare feet crossed the bedroom, and Emma Kate turned the light back on. Ruf made his way back to bed, holding down his shirt tail.

"There's an extra light bulb up there in the safe, Birdie," Emma Kate said wearily. "First though, get me a wet washrag with some soap on it, and bring it in here. "I'll jest wait till the signs get right again to wean Dolfus."

"I hate for you to have to do that, Emma Kate," Ruf said from among the covers. "But I bodaciously need to get some sleep. I'd hate to get cut to jiblets. It won't be long till the signs are right again."

"Can we have the nanners, Mama?" Eva Jane asked as Birdie got the bulb screwed in. "Can we?"

"Yes, you'uns can have them. Now you'uns divide them equal."

Again there came the sound of scuffling in the kitchen. Then Birdie spoke triumphantly. "I'll divide 'em. There's three besides the half. We'll save the half for Dolfus."

"I'm gonna have the half," Ned announced.

"No you ain't, Ned Alvester! You make my blood run cold, you hog, you!"

"Birdie!" Ruf roared, "didn't I tell you not to let me hear you say that 'blood run cold' again?"

"She says it all the time," Eva Jane said.

"She got it from Sweetie Foster," Ned added.

"She better not let me hear her say it again," Ruf warned.

After that the house fell into an uneasy quiet.

The Eaters

Bird-Eye Donker's feet hit the plank floor of his two-room shanty shortly after daylight broke over Halltree County. It was the second Sunday in July, Homecoming Day at Macedonia Baptist Church, and the Donkers attended all homecomings, reunions, and memorial days within a radius of twenty-five miles; sometimes they ranged even farther. They brought away enough victuals from these events to keep their stomachs quiet for a week at a time.

"Git up, Jensie!" Bird-Eye shouted. "You gonna sleep all day? Dag-nabit woman, we got to hurry!"

Jensie roused and sat up on the side of the bed, her hair in a wild tangle. "Gimme dipa snuff," she said. "Hit ain't mor'n six miles over there, Bird-Eye. You aiming to git thar 'fore the preacher?"

"Naw," Bird-Eye replied, pulling a smooth worn snuffbox out of his britches pocket, handing it to his wife reluctantly. "Dag-nabit, Jensie, I believe you're crazy! You know we got to allow time for flats."

Jensie pulled her lower lip out and shook snuff into it.

"Don't use all that snuff!" Bird-Eye hollered.

"Ahm not go use it awl," Jensie mouthed, arranging the snuff with her tongue. She handed the box back. "Git the chillern up."

Bird-Eye looked into the snuffbox, then closed and pocketed it. He walked over to the other bed in the room and shook the foot of it.

Two wormy-looking, stringy-haired kids, a boy and a girl, leaped out of bed like grasshoppers. They had slept in their clothes, and

Tillie, the girl, who was eight and the oldest, began trying to rub out the wrinkles in her print flour sack dress. The skirt struck the child's bony legs halfway between her knees and ankles, and was fringed and raveling around the edges. Jensie had made the dress by hand and decided there was no sense in hemming it. Spider took a running start and turned a somersault in the middle of the bed, landed on his feet on the other side, and broke wind.

"Pa, Spider pooted!" Tillie reported indignantly.

"Dag-nabit, boy," Bird-Eye warned, "You better learn to hold that wind!"

"Now Bird-Eye he can't help breaking wind," Jensie bristled.

"He better not let me hear him breaking wind at that homecoming. He can hold it back over there. He gits back home I don't care if he plays a tune!"

Jensie got up and pulled a faded yellow dress on over the slip she'd slept in. "Git a bucket of water, Bird-Eye," she said, "while I make a far in the stove." She rummaged in the big old fireplace and found some paper and other trash and went into the side room that served as a kitchen. Cramming the paper and trash into the stove, she lit it, poked in a few sticks of stove wood, and put the coffeepot on to boil.

Bird-Eye went out to the well and let the bucket down. The day was fresh washed after the rain in the night. Observing the field of stunted corn on the rocky hillside back of his house Bird-Eye muttered, "Grass has jest about taken that corn, spite of all me and Jensie and the chillern can do. Dag-nabit, I shore ain't got no time to help Old Man Bailey out with his haying."

He caught the brimming bucket of water as it came up and poured it into the one he'd brought from the kitchen. He spit at a bumblebee, thinking how lucky he was to have the homecomings, reunions, and memorial days to fall back on for victuals to feed himself and his family.

Back in the kitchen Bird-Eye poured water into a leaky washpan on the rickety table beside the door. After splashing water on his face, he dried it and then combed his hair with his fingers, looking into a cracked mirror that hung on the wall above the table. Blind in one eye as the result of a free-for-all family fight before he was good grown,

Bird-Eye's expression seemed to imply that he had simply closed one eye and hadn't yet decided to open it.

A molting Rhode Island Red hen came stepping cautiously into the kitchen.

"Shoo-OO!" Bird-Eye yelled, flapping the sack towel at her. "Dag-nabit, old Mattie, you better start laying some eggs or you're gonna end up et!"

"Naw, Pa!" Tillie screeched, "we're not gon' eat Mattie!"

"Bird-Eye, I wisht you'd stop talking about eatin' Mattie," Jensie fussed, setting a pone of leftover cornbread on the table. "We et up all them other chickens Mis' Bailey give us, but the chillern's took sech a liking to Mattie we can't eat her and you know it!"

"Wal, hit'll shore look bad we starve to death with a big old fat hen waddling around here."

He couldn't stay cross long, however, not with thoughts of the Macedonia Homecoming hopping and skipping around in his head. There'd be food enough on that picnic table to make a dead man rise. He opened up the old-fashioned icebox and put in a hand to check its coolness. There had been a special trip to Mintersville the day before to buy a hundred pounds of ice so the icebox would be ready for the Macedonia Homecoming haul. Bird-Eye jumped up and clicked his heels together.

Jensie poured the pale, boiled-over coffee into four mismatched cups, two of which had no handles, but Bird-Eye had a saucer, and they sat down to drink it with the cornbread.

"You reckon Mr. Bailey got all his hay in yestiddy?" Jensie asked. "If he didn't, that rain last night ruint it."

"Yeah, I guess it got ruint alright," Bird-Eye agreed. "But I shore couldn't help him. I had to go to town atter that ice fer the icebox."

"Did he act like he was mad 'cause you couldn't help him?"

"Mad enough to eat fried chicken!" Bird-Eye laughed uproariously at his joke and blew on the coffee in his saucer.

"He told some the men at Chalmer's Store you was too lazy to work and he's gonna put a stop to us bringing victuals away from the church on homecomin' day," Jensie said.

"Ole Brad wouldn't do that. Anyway, I'd like to know how he'd stop us." He reared back in his chair with a daring grin. "It's a free country."

A dirt dauber razzed away, building his mud nest on a rafter overhead, and the songs of the mockingbirds could be heard through the open windows. Bird-Eye got out the cardboard boxes they used for their hauls and put them in the back of the pickup truck. At eight o'clock they pulled out, popping and smoking.

Their faces were clean, and Jensie wore a red geranium in her combed-out black hair. On her feet she wore a pair of once-white tennis shoes with a hole cut out to accommodate the corn on her right little toe. She was thirty and much stronger looking than Bird-Eye. Tillie's sulphur-colored hair, cut by Jensie so that it just topped her ears, was parted in the middle and combed down straight on both sides. She had a strand of dime store beads, big as marbles, around her skinny little neck. Someone had given her an outsized woman's purse, and it hung heavily on one small arm.

Spider wore short pants made from a pair of old striped trousers Mrs. Bailey gave him. They were so tight, the boy looked as if he were being constantly jerked upwards. Bird-Eye's britches, shapeless and bagging in the seat, were some Boss Jackson gave him when he thought Bird-Eye was going to help him mend his pasture fence.

Half a mile past Ledlowe Creek Bridge, the tire on the left front wheel of the pickup went flat. Muttering complaints, Bird-Eye got his old jack and went to work. He pried the tire off, found the hole in the inner tube, and called for his patching kit. Jensie and the kids got out of the truck to stand in the shade of a sweet gum tree growing beside the road, watching Bird-Eye work.

He had his back to them, and in a few minutes Jensie, who still had drifts of romance about her, said, "Bird-Eye, I wisht you'd git you some britches that fit."

"Dag-nabit, Jensie, I wisht you'd keep yore tongue still! I'm about to burn up fixing this tar and you're talkin' about fittin' britches!" He swiped the perspiration off his brow with his hand and took a reading on the sun.

"Pa, Spider pooted again!" Tillie reported.

"Shet up!" Jensie slapped at her. "Yore Pa's busy. Stop hinderin' him!"

A late-model car came into view down the road and slowed to a stop as it reached them. It was Rodney Bailey. He hailed them heartily. "Hello, Bird-Eye, you got trouble?"

"I shore have, Rodney. Old tar went flat. Bout got'er fixed though."

"Did yore Pa git his hay in yestiddy, Rodney?" Jensie asked.

"Not all of it. Some of it got wet. He's mad as a jersey bull!"

"Ain't you going to the homecomin', Rodney?" Bird-Eye asked, changing the subject quickly. "You're heading the wrong way."

"I'm going all right!" Rodney laughed. "But I've got to go git my girl first. Miss Lillou Barton!" He slapped both hands onto the steering wheel, let out a whoop, and drove off.

Bird-Eye threw the jack into the back of the pickup and climbed in. "Dag-nabit, Jensie," he fumed, "I wisht you'd learn to keep yore trap shut!" He stomped down on the gas pedal as they approached the Bailey place, and they went by it in a blur.

Arriving at Macedonia Baptist Church by 9:30, Bird-Eye parked his truck in the shade of a majestic elm tree. There were only a few scattered cars on the church grounds at that hour. The owners of these were inside conducting Sunday School. There would be no preaching. After a fracas that nearly split the church, those opposed to preaching on homecoming day had outvoted those who wanted it, and that was that. The majority of the homecomers would come around 11:30.

The Donkers sat patiently in the old pickup, trying to look nonchalant. They felt a twinge of uneasiness. The kids picked at each other a little. Tillie hit Spider over the head with her purse, and he hollered, "Stop!"

"Dag-nabit, you chillern git quiet!" Bird-Eye ordered in an undertone, gritting his teeth.

Slowly the churchyard filled up with all makes and models of cars. Rodney rolled in with Lillou sitting close beside him. He parked not far from the Donkers' pickup, and he and Lillou got out. Rodney threw up a hand at Bird-Eye and his family as they walked by.

Slender as a fishing pole, Lillou was a gift package in a lime-green organdy dress, with a mass of short windblown brown hair. She bounced as she walked along beside Rodney, her face full of laughter.

Bird-Eye got a whiff of Lillou's perfume and wished he did have a pair of britches that fit. "Old Rodney's feeling his oats," he chuckled, reaching over to chuck Jensie under the chin.

She hit at his hand. "Fool!" she snapped. "There's Mr. Bailey and Mis' Bailey," she went on with hardly a pause. "He shore looks mad!"

"He most always looks mad," Bird-Eye said.

"I saw him shootin' a look over here at us."

"Let him shoot," Bird-Eye dismissed the subject airily.

A little after 12 o'clock the people inside the church began coming out. The Donkers joined the crowd around the long picnic table, mingling in unobtrusively. Baskets and boxes of food were brought from the trunks of cars by the men and set down beside the table, and the women took it from there. Each woman set her food on a section of the table, after first spreading out a tablecloth she'd brought. Some of those who lived close enough to the church went home to fetch their dinner after services broke. These didn't have much choice about where they'd spread. Most though, by an unspoken assent, chose the same section year after year.

Rodney brought the large basket of food from his father's car and set it down a little to the right of the table's center for his mother. She put on the snowy white tablecloth and set out a great platter of sliced baked ham.

The Donkers locked eyes. Bird-Eye rolled his eyes in the direction of his pickup, and the others read him clearly. Some of that ham would help make up the day's haul.

Brad Bailey came through the crowd with a big bag of cracked ice that would be used to cool whatever the women had brought to drink. He passed close to Bird-Eye before Bird-Eye could retreat and paused to glare at him. "Hay got wet!" Brad Bailey threw the words out like ammunition and moved on while Bird-Eye blinked his one eye sheepishly.

Bird-Eye and his family eased their way to another part of the table.

All down the length of the thirty-yard-long table the women's hands moved in a rhythm like weavers or dancers, as they leaned down to their boxes and baskets and came up with platters, bowls, plates, jars, and pans of such delectable victuals as women have made for homecomings over many years.

When they were finished, the old plank table had blossomed into a delicious-smelling, mouthwatering wonder. Crisp fried chicken, crusty brown and fluffy cornbread dressing, chicken dumplings, baked hams, chicken pies, fresh vegetables of every kind, including fried corn and fried okra. There were deviled eggs and candied sweet potatoes. When it came to desserts the women had tried to outdo each other. Luscious coconut cakes, chocolate cakes, caramel cakes, carrot cakes, lemon and butterscotch pies piled three inches high with meringue, golden egg custards sprinkled lavishly with nutmeg, pound cakes, and jelly rolls nodded to each other up and down the table. Potato salad, cucumber pickles, sliced tomatoes, and hot peppers graced nearly every family's section.

When everything was ready someone clapped for attention, and a hush fell over the crowd as the Macedonia pastor asked the blessing. After that it was eating time.

Big black ants scurried up and down the legs of the picnic table, bent on taking advantage of the occasion. People slapped at them, some squeaked at them, but this didn't hinder the plate-filling. Sweat bees dealt misery to bare arms. The steady flow of talk never faltered as friends and relatives visited with each other and ate.

Bird-Eye and his family kept together. They eased in to the table, and Jensie filled two plates for Tillie and Spider. They moved off eating. Bird-Eye heaped his plate with fried chicken, roast beef, fried corn, chicken dumplings, deviled eggs, and candied potatoes and had gone back up against the church house to devour it when Jensie joined him with a full plate of her own.

Leaning over close to his wife, Bird-Eye said in a low voice, with his mouth full and going fast, "You see that pile of ham Mis' Bailey set out, Jensie? I'm a gittin' me soma that to take home."

Jensie swallowed a big bite of egg custard and said, as soon as she could speak, "Mr. Bailey's mad, Bird-Eye. You'd best keep clear of him and his victuals. He's liable to take out atter us."

"Old Brad ain't go do nothing," Bird-Eye said, cleaning a drumstick.

"Pa, Spider pooted again," Tillie reported as she and Spider came up to their parents.

"Boy!" Bird-Eye grabbed Spider's arm and jerked him up close to glare at him with his one good eye. Two deviled eggs fell off his plate. He let go of Spider and took both hands to his plate. "I'm a gonna take a board to you, boy, I hear of you doing that again!"

"He can't help it, Bird-Eye," Jensie said, without missing a bite.

Bird-Eye had gone back to the table, motioning Spider and Tillie to follow him. They slipped through the chattering crowd, Bird-Eye filling their plates. By the time they had gone one-fourth the length of the table, the children's plates were heaped with fried chicken and roast beef. Bird-Eye cleared his throat, and they left the table heading for the pickup.

When Spider and Tillie were back at the table Jensie slipped out with a plateful of coconut cake and lemon meringue pie. Bird-Eye made off with a big ration of chicken dressing. And so it was, working together like this, the Donkers stashed a portion of nearly every dish on the table.

They were standing against the church house, eating again, when Bird-Eye said, "Jensie, you and the chillern go on and git in the truck. I'm a gonna git me a plate of Mis' Bailey's ham, and I reckon we'll be ready to go."

"Bird-Eye," Jensie said, "I'm a telling you, you better leave that ham alone. We done already got some ham. Mr. Bailey's watching you!"

"Git on in the truck, Jensie. I wudden born yestiddy." He chuckled.

Jensie and the children headed for the truck. Bird-Eye ambled back to the picnic table. The homecomers were about finished with eating, and everybody was talking. Nobody paid much attention to who got what. It was considered a compliment when someone asked for part of another person's dish. And though it irked them for the Donkers to freeload, they didn't really care all that much.

That is, as a rule they didn't. But today Brad Bailey was boiling mad. Every time he thought of his ruined hay he wanted to hit Bird-Eye Donker.

Bird-Eye had most of what was left of Mis' Bailey's ham and was moseying out to the pickup when a roar shattered the Macedonia Homecoming harmony. Brad Bailey broke from the crowd bellowing, "Bring that ham back here, you lazy low-life thief! I been watching you steal that food! This is one time you're not gonna get away with it!"

"Yea, yea!" Boss Jackson whooped. "Go get him, Brad! Sorry lying rascal!"

Mis' Bailey screamed, "Stop your Pa, Rodney!"

Bird-Eye sprang forward at the first roar, threw the plate into one of the open boxes, and had the pickup cranked and in gear in thirty seconds. He scratched off with a shower of dirt and left the Macedonia church grounds, popping like a machine gun. Jensie and the children grabbed whatever they could find to hold onto as Bird-Eye leveled off.

"He's atter us!" Jensie screamed.

Bird-Eye bent to the steering wheel, his jaw set with a grim determination as he floorboarded the gas pedal. Simon-pure panic enveloped the occupants of the old pickup truck as it sped on up the road. The kids bounced wildly but made no sound except when one would yell, "I see him coming!" Presently Spider hollered, "I see Rodney's car. He's atter us too!"

"He's atter his Pa!" Bird-Eye shouted. "Hand me soma that ham up here!" He kept his eye on the road and his foot on the gas pedal.

Holding on with one hand, Spider swung around and grabbed at the ham. Catching a fist full he swung back and passed it to Bird-Eye. Bird-Eye crammed his mouth full.

"Hand me some coconut cake!"

"Bird-Eye, have you gone crazy?" Jensie screamed.

"Naw! I'm ona eat this grub up 'fore old Brad Bailey gits a crumb of it. Gimme some chicken!"

Jensie, swaying and bouncing, got up on her knees in the seat of the pickup, facing backward and yelling to the kids to hand her one of the boxes. Staggering, swinging back and forth, they got the box to her. She handed them both a hunk of beef roast and began gobbling chicken dressing herself.

"He's gaining on us, Pa!" Spider hollered. "I can hear his car horn, and he's shaking his fist out the window. Rodney's a comin' too!"

Bird-Eye put both hands on the steering wheel and pumped the gas pedal. He called for more food, opened his mouth for Jensie to feed him, and got choked. Jensie beat him on the back. The food went down. Tillie had candied potatoes in her hair. Spider's face was plastered with lemon meringue pie. Grease dripped off Jensie's chin.

"Pa, Spider pooted!" Tillie leaned forward to shout.

"Shet up, Tille!" Bird-Eye hollerd. "I don't keer if he blows the seat out'en his britches! Jensie! Dag-nabit, woman, git some more that ham in my mouth!"

And so the cars sped on out Halltree County Road Number 5, with the Donkers consuming victuals in a frantic effort to get them all inside their bellies before Brad Bailey overtook them. Rodney, with Lillou beside him, was doing his best to catch his Pa before his Pa overtook Bird-Eye, while Boss Jackson in his car a long with two other cars, whose drivers were anticipating entertainment, followed Rodney, neither gaining nor losing ground.

Man Is Head of Woman

His name was Ephraim Kinnard, and we called him Uncle Eef, though he was not really our uncle. He was no kin to us at all, and nobody around our parts knew where he came from. He'd stay a spell with one family, and then pick up and go stay awhile with someone else. It was not uncommon for him to have a run-in with some member of a family that would end in his sudden departure to visit elsewhere.

He liked to spout off about "man being head of woman," and this kept lots of the women mad at him. He didn't care about that though. He'd come in and make himself at home like he'd been invited, and like as not he would start bossing.

Me and my little sister Mary Lee was out on our front porch one July morning trying to catch a bumblebee in a morning glory blossom, when Mary Lee looked up and said, "Yonder comes Uncle Eef!" We forgot about the bumblebee and sat down on the front porch to wait for him.

He was a small man and always wore clothes that were three sizes too big for him. He carried all his possessions around with him in a burlap sack, and he thought nothing of tossing his dirty shirt and britches, without apology, into the family wash when he was visiting. Sometimes when he'd leave in a hurry, he would gather his clothes off the clothesline as he left. His sparse white hair always blew about on his head like thistles in a breeze. He never failed to ask Ma to cut his hair when he visited us.

Even with his burlap sack and his flapping britches and his turned-in toes, there was still a kind of dignity about him as he came plodding up the road. I think he stayed at our house more than he stayed anywhere else. I don't know why 'cause Pa was pretty fractious with him sometimes.

"Good morning, children," he greeted us as he came up the walk to the front steps. We saw he had a small bundle of wood he'd gathered along the road, in addition to his sack. This was a habit of his. I guess he thought it would please the women, and they wouldn't mind his visiting. "And why are you brats not helping your parents on this fine day?"

"We're resting!" Mary Lee said in a sassy tone of voice. She was eight years old, and I was ten.

"Resting from what, may I ask?" Uncle Eef inquired as he came up the steps and put his sack down.

"From picking bugs off the potatoes!" I snapped.

We liked to have company no matter who it was, but you can see why we were not exactly crazy about Uncle Eef. He really did like to boss when it wasn't none of his business.

He went on in the kitchen, and we followed him. Throwing the wood down, he did a fancy bow and said to Ma, "Good day, Madam. I see you are busy preparing toothsome provender for your family. It's my pleasure to salute your gilded virtues."

"Good morning, Eef." Ma didn't even look up from the pie crust she was rolling.

"Where's Homer?" Uncle Eef asked.

"He's piddling around out at the barn, I think," Ma said.

Uncle Eef left for the barn.

Ma sighed. She washed her hands and put a piece of Uncle Eef's wood in the stove. "I wish that old codger wouldn't come around here when your Pa's at loose ends," she said, more to herself than to us.

Pa had laid-by his crop, and time was a little heavy on his hands. He had been fishing twice but was tired of it. Ma suggested cutting firewood for winter, but Pa scoffed and said he didn't intend to cut firewood when the weather was hotter'n hell. He said it wasn't natural. So he just hung around the barn straightening up his harnesses and sharpening his tools.

Ma called dinner, and when we were seated and had helped our plates, Ma asked, "How are the Crocketts, Eef?" She knew he'd come from a visit with them.

"Madam," Uncle Eef said, sitting up very straight and pausing with a spoonful of corn on the way to his mouth, "It behooves me to inform you that Maybell Crockett is as void of intelligence as a hen turkey."

I could see Ma bristle a little. "Why?" She asked. "What happened?"

"I gave her eldest son a dose of Epsom salts while they were away visiting," Uncle Eef said.

"You just took it on yourself to give the child a dose of Epsom salts, did you?" Ma's voice had gone up a notch.

"Was he sick?" Pa asked.

"Homer, I know when a child needs a dose of Epsom salts, whether he has any symptoms or not. The boy was pale and shaky."

Pa laughed. "I bet he got pale and shaky after you mentioned giving him a dose of Epsom salts, Eef."

"And I suppose it made Maybell Crockett mad," Ma said.

"It made her wroth, Madam, absolutely wroth! She suggested I leave their premises."

"Well I certainly don't blame her!" Ma exploded.

"Man is head of woman," Uncle Eef declared.

Ma just sat there and glared at him.

After dinner Pa and Uncle Eef took their chairs and went out to sit in the shade of our chinaberry tree. When Ma finished cleaning up the kitchen, with our help, she decided to lie down and rest awhile before she started canning peaches. That left Mary Lee and me free to do as we pleased, so we went down to the ditch and tried to catch crawdads. That didn't last long, though, 'cause the crawdads outsmarted us, and we came back and laid down on the watermelon table under the chinaberry tree. I dozed off I guess, then all at once I heard Uncle Eef say, "Why don't we make us a run of white lightening, Homer?"

"Shucks," Pa said, "What are you tawkin' about, Eef? We ain't got no still to make no whiskey."

"Hop Hawkins would lend us the use of his any day. You and Hop are good friends, are you not?"

"Yeah." Pa pushed back his hat (he wore it all the time) and scratched his head. "I-dog," he said after about a minute had passed, "we might could do it."

Hop Hawkins was the whiskey man of Pinetucky Beat. He moved his still constantly so as to dodge the revenue men. Most of the women despised him, but the whiskey-drinking men swore by old Hop.

"He has moved his still to the heart of Mulberry Creek swamp," Uncle Eef informed Pa. "He will have no fear our whiskey-making fever will endanger his regular business."

Pa laughed and slapped his leg.

Me and Mary Lee didn't lose any time telling Ma what we'd heard. She didn't say a word or bat an eye. I kind of wisht we hadn't told her, but I knowed she was bound to find out anyway.

I guess she must have brooded over it all afternoon, and by supper time she couldn't hold back any longer. "So you're going to make some whiskey, are you?" She blurted out to Pa.

"Whiskey maketh a merry heart," Uncle Eef spoke up.

Pa shot a glance at him, then at me and Mary Lee. Then he reached over and patted Ma's hand and said soothingly, "Now, Julie." Pa usually did as he pleased, so I guess she thought there was no use starting a ruckus. She held her tongue.

Next morning things were glum. At the breakfast table Uncle Eef passed his cup for coffee, and Pa, who always kept the coffeepot sitting on the floor beside him, picked it up and started pouring. When the cup was no more than half full, Uncle Eef hollered, "Whoa!"

He always did this, and it infuriated Pa 'cause he knew Uncle Eef would be passing his cup for more coffee in less than two minutes. So when he hollered whoa, Pa just kept pouring till he ran the cup over, with Uncle Eef getting louder and louder.

"Whoa! Whoa! My God, man, whoa I say!"

This happened every time Uncle Eef came to visit, and me and Mary Lee somehow knew it wouldn't be a good idea to laugh. This morning we didn't even want to laugh.

Hop Hawkins lived about a mile down the road from us, and as soon as breakfast was over Pa went off in that direction. When he came back, him and Uncle Eef shelled a shopping turn of corn and took it to the gristmill. Late that afternoon they cleaned up the oaken barrel Pa used at hog-killing time to scald the porkers and carried it, along with the meal, out behind the barn.

Me and Mary Lee wanted in the worst kind of way to get out there and see what they were doing, but Ma threatened to blister us if she caught us so much as looking out that way. Finally she went to milk the cows, and we followed her, hoping to get a little closer to Pa and Uncle Eef.

As we went in the cow stall, they were going around the barn, not knowing we were anywhere near. "Well, that takes care of the mash," Pa said.

"You are fortunate to have me to advise you in the making of this beverage, Homer," Uncle Eef bragged.

"Hell!" Pa snorted, "I know how to make corn whiskey!"

Ma went right on cooking and washing dishes like she always did, and she kept me and Mary Lee busy bringing in water and stove wood and picking bugs off the potatoes, but there was thunder in the air. Pa tried to treat Ma courtly. He hoed two rows in the garden that didn't need hoeing, and he was uncommonly jolly. Uncle Eef stayed out of Ma's way except at the table, and then he would brag on her cooking. Ma spoke, very politely, only when it was necessary.

You could tell Pa was fed up with all the unwanted advice Uncle Eef insisted on giving him. When the hogs got into the mash the next day after they added the sugar, Uncle Eef advised Pa to knock all the hogs in the head on the spot.

"You're tawking like a fool, Ephraim Kinnard," Pa said. "That's my next winter's meat."

"Hog meat is an abomination to the Almighty, Homer."

"Now you're tawkin like a damn rabbi!" Pa snapped. "What are you, some kind of Jew?"

"No, Homer, but I've assisted and advised some top-knocking rabbis in my time. They know I'm a friend that sticketh tighter than a brother. The Jews are God's chosen, you know."

"Hell!" Pa snorted. "You wouldn't know a rabbi from a raccoon! Anyways," he went on without taking a new breath, "I ain't noticed you turnin' down any hog meat. You can eat more ham than a holy-roller preacher!"

"It has always been my understanding that preachers eat chicken," Uncle Eef said.

Pa didn't say another word. He just went stomping off to start another barrel of mash.

Ma kept threatening to switch me and Mary Lee if we didn't stay away from behind the barn. "Jesse, you and Mary Lee mind yore Ma," Pa said. "You ain't got no business messin' around grown-ups' affairs anyway."

So we laid low, but we kept our eyes and ears open.

Sunday came, and Pa went to church with us, which was something he didn't usually do. He looked so dandy in his striped britches and yellow shirt, with his thick black hair and his broad shoulders and skinny hips. I felt proud of him. Ma was so pleased she softened up a mite and smiled and talked a little. But that didn't last long.

On the following Wednesday, Ma had Mary Lee and me on the back porch snapping cornfield beans to can. Pa and Uncle Eef came around the house and sat down on a bench by the well curb. I motioned Mary Lee to be quiet.

"Well, that mash is ready again for the sugar," we heard Pa say. "So I guess I'll have to go to the store this afternoon."

"There's no need for you to make that trip to the store," Uncle Eef said. "Your wife has ten pounds of sugar laid-by in the back of her pantry."

"She's got that sugar saved for making watermelon rind preserves," Pa said. "She'd scob my nob if I was to slip that sugar and use it."

"Man is head of woman," Uncle Eef declared.

"Well then, you go get it," Pa said, "since you know so much about it."

About that time Ma broke out to banging pots and pans in the kitchen, and our brindle cat came streaking out the back door mewing and spittin' like he'd seen old Nick. Ma was mad as usual.

"Poor woman, she's out of sorts," we heard Uncle Eef say. "You'd best go to the store for the sugar."

After they added the sugar to the mash, Pa sharpened his crosscut saw, and him and Uncle Eef cut and hauled a load of firewood and stacked it in the woodhouse. They tightened up Ma's clothesline and brought some leaf mould from the woods for her flowerpots.

Mary Lee and me finally got a chance to sneak out behind the barn to take a peek in that barrel. Whew! The smell of it gave us a jolt. We couldn't be satisfied till we tasted it, so I found a gourd dipper hanging back there, and we took a sip. It tasted good! Sweet and tangy. About that time we heard Ma calling us, so we skedaddled.

At last the day came when the mash had fermented and was ready for the still. Pa and Uncle Eef loaded the barrel onto our two-horse wagon. Pa had rounded up what few jugs he could find about the place, but for fear these might not hold all the whiskey in the run, he decided to carry along a big-mouthed five-gallon milk can. They piled on hay to cover the nature of what they were hauling, hitched up the mules, and left for Mulberry Creek swamp.

Me and Mary Lee wanted to go so bad we cried, but Ma threatened to jerk a knot in us, so we hushed up and went to lie down on the velvety moss under our beech tree where we could hear the ditch water gurgle. Mr. Babcock, the mailman, saw us and waved at us when he stopped to put the mail in our mailbox. Mr. Babcock was a kindly, solemn man. We liked him. Sometimes he would give us a piece of gum when we'd race to see who could get the daily newspaper first. Today neither of us made a move.

"Are you children sick?" Mr. Babcock called out to us.

"Naw, sir."

He drove on.

Ma washed clothes in the morning, and she made watermelon rind preserves all that long hot July afternoon, but she let us loaf. It was a strange time. I was surprised when I saw her hang out Uncle Eef's shirt and britches. I'd never seen her hang britches like that before. She hung them upside down with the legs spread as far apart as she could get them. I wondered if she was pretending she was hanging up Uncle Eef.

Night came and then bedtime. Pa and Uncle Eef were still gone. Me and Mary Lee went to sleep. They woke us up singing. Pa was singing "Froggie Went a Courtin," while Uncle Eef sang "You Take the High Road." Uncle Eef's voice would jump the track and go up to a screech when he rightly needed a low note.

"Shut up!" Pa shouted as they came back around the house after taking the jugs to the smokehouse. "You sound worse'n a dog in a yellow jacket nest!"

"Homer, a man of your station can scarcely be expected to appreciate opry."

"Opry, hell!" Pa snorted. "You wouldn't know opry if you met him in the middle of the road! I think you're drunk."

"Corn whiskey maketh a merry heart," Uncle Eef said and went back to singing. He cut off long enough to add, "Don't overlook your own inebriation, my man."

We heard Ma get out of bed and head for the front porch. Me and Mary Lee crept silently behind her. All at once Uncle Eef cut off singing again. Ma had reached the porch.

"Behold, your bride cometh, Homer!" Uncle Eef proclaimed.

Ma just stood there. I guess she was too mad to speak.

"Why, Julie," Pa said like he was talking to a little child. "You orter be in bed asleep. Did we wake you up?"

"No! I have not been asleep." The way she said it made me think of slashing hay with a scythe.

"Man ish head of woman," Uncle Eef said, heading back to the wagon.

"I-dog, Eef," Pa hollered, "you're fixing to get your stupid head knocked off!" Then he turned to Ma and said, "Go on back to bed, Julie. I'll be there in a minute."

"Don't you come in this house tonight, Homer Foster." Ma didn't holler, but there was no mistaking what she said. "You nor that ... that creature you've got helping you make whiskey. I'll shoot you both if you set foot in this house!"

"Now, Julie ...."

Ma whirled and came back in the house. She got Pa's double-barreled twelve-gauge shotgun from the rack and took it to bed with her. We had never seen Ma that mad.

Pa and Uncle Eef put the five-gallon milk can on the front porch, and after that I reckon they went to sleep in the barn.

When I woke up and went to the kitchen the next morning, I was surprised to find Pa and Uncle Eef already seated at the table and Ma bringing on a plate of biscuits. But I soon saw all was not well. Pa and Uncle Eef had already had a few drinks. I could smell it, and I could tell by the way they were both acting—real agreeable and a little cocky. The best way I could gauge the situation, though, was by looking at Ma. Her lips were pressed together so tight her nose and chin were not far apart. She never said a word.

As soon as breakfast was over, the two men headed for the front porch. Me and Mary Lee followed them. Uncle Eef was dipping into the big-mouthed can with the dipper from our front porch water bucket.

As soon as Pa saw us he said, "You young'uns get around yonder and feed them chickens." He reached for the dipper.

We went through the hallway to the backyard and just stood there. We don't feed our chickens in the morning. Ma passed us going to milk the cows. She never spoke.

"Jesse," Mary Lee said, "I'm scared."

"Me too."

She began to cry. "Aw, don't cry," I said. "Come on, let's slip under the porch and listen."

As soon as we got under the porch, we heard Pa saying, "Gimme that dipper, Eef. You're gonna git tanked again."

"Are you inferring that I can't handle my whiskey?" Uncle Eef demanded.

"I shore am!" Pa snapped. "You was drunk as a boiled owl last night. I-dog, I think maybe I orter not made this stuff. I ain't never seen Julie so put out."

"Man is head of woman," Uncle Eef droned.

"Hell!" Pa exploded, "What do you know about woman? You ain't never had a woman to be head of!"

"Little you know, my man, little you know! In my time I've laid suit to some of the most exotic women of the world."

"What kind's them?" Pa asked.

"Varigated."

They both laughed uproariously. All this time we could hear the dipper clanking as they'd dip it in the milk can.

"I've got to go take a leak," Pa said. We heard his footsteps going through the house. While he was gone, the mailman came. Right after we heard Mr. Babcock's car coming up the road, we heard the dipper clank and Uncle Eef said, "I expect that poor man would appreciate something to wet his whistle." And with that he came down the steps.

While he had his back turned going toward the mailbox, we came from under the porch and ran and got under the chinaberry tree.

Uncle Eef reached the mailbox, holding the dipper very carefully, as Mr. Babcock drove up and stopped. "Good morning Eef," Mr. Babcock said as he put our mail in the box.

"And a hearty good morning to you, Babcock!" Uncle Eef boomed out, extending the dipper. "Have a drink, sir."

Mr. Babcock could certainly smell the stuff, besides seeing that Uncle Eef was near drunk. "Thank you, Eef," he said, "but it's against the law for me to drink on the job."

"Oh tish, man," Uncle Eef insisted, "come on and have a drink. One drink can do you no damage. Besides, the law won't know about it." He pressed the dipper on Mr. Babcock.

"No, Eef, I can't drink on the job."

"Man!" Uncle Eef yelled. "The Bible says 'drink and be merry.' Who do you intend to obey, the Bible or the law?"

Mr. Babcock laughed.

I guess that laugh jolted Uncle Eef the wrong way. All at once he brought the dipper to his own lips and drank the whiskey himself. Then in a flash he whacked Mr. Babcock over the head with the empty dipper. We heard it pop. "All right then!" he shouted. "If you can't drink my whiskey, don't you ever dare put another piece of mail in my mailbox!"

Just then Pa shouted from the porch. "Ephraim Kinnard, that ain't yore mailbox! Whadda you mean treatin' Babcock in sech a way? I'm a good mind to knock yore head off!"

"Have you no pride, Homer?" Uncle Eef inquired politely as he came back up the walk swinging the dipper. "The man insulted us grievously."

"Damn you, Eef," Pa hollered, coming down the steps. "You ain't nothin' but a pigeon-toed busybody!" He was balling and unballing his fists. "Taking other people's business on yoreself to tend to like it was your'n!"

Pa was lots bigger than Uncle Eef, but Uncle Eef was game, especially with all that booze in his belly, and I think they'd have gone together if Hop Hawkins hadn't drove up right then in his spanking new Model-T Ford. He cut off the motor, and him and Jake Tankersly got out. Old Tank was Hop's assistant bootlegger.

"Howdy, neighbors," Hop greeted them. "How's she this morning?" Hop was a dandified fellow with patent leather shoes and slicked-down yellow hair and a shifty look. I think he was trying to be dapper, meaning the world in general, by saying "she." But Ma had come out on the porch, and I knowed she'd took it that he meant her. I guess that fanned her anger to a fury. She popped back into the house.

"She's fine, Hop," Uncle Eef bandied. "Fine and fancy. Would you gentlemen join us in a drink?"

"Aw, naw." Hop started to speak.

"Come on, have a drink," Pa said. You could tell he was still piffed at Uncle Eef.

Hop laughed. "Might as well," he said.

They went up on the porch and started clanking the dipper and passing it around.

Pa noticed us standing under the chinaberry tree. "Jesse, you and Mary Lee git out yonder and bug the potatoes," he ordered.

Going around the house we came in at the back door. We had no intention of bugging the potatoes. In the front room we found Ma with Pa's gun across her lap and Uncle Eef's burlap sack on the floor beside her. She was puffed up like a bull snake, and her face was white as a lily.

The dipper clanking on the front porch went on, and we could hear the men talking. It wasn't long till Pa said, "I-dog, Hop, my wife's mad at me."

Hop and Tankersly laughed real loud.

"Man is head of woman."

Ma sprang out of her chair with the gun across one arm and Uncle Eef's sack in one hand. She marched out onto the porch, put the sack down, and kicked it across the porch.

There was absolute silence.

Then Uncle Eef spoke, "Git back in the house Mish Foster. This ish not a female party."

The gun clicked as Ma brought the stock up to her shoulder and cocked it.

"I want you men to leave here," Ma said.

Hop and Old Tank nearly fell down the steps and sprinted for the car. They clawed the door open with Hop screaming, "Crank it, Tank, crank it!" Tank ran to the front and jerked wildly till it cranked. He dived in, and they left.

"You too, Ephraim Kinnard," Ma said, stamping her foot. "Get going!"

Looking awfully offended, Uncle Eef picked up his sack and started down the steps. He stopped and looked back up at Pa. "Homer," he said, "are you going to allow this woman to nol-pros your bosom friend?"

Boom! Pa's double-barreled twelve-gauge shotgun went off. Ma had fired it, not at Uncle Eef, but at his britches hanging spread-legged on the clothesline where she'd hung them the day before. One leg was shot clean in two, and there they dangled by the other leg.

"Madam," Uncle Eef said slowly, staring in disbelief. "You've ruined my britches."

"You'd better git em and git out from here," Ma said as she cocked the gun again, "before I ruin that pair you've got on! I'll show you who is head of who, you old pustle-gut!" She brought the stock to her shoulder again.

Uncle Eef sprang into action. Clutching his burlap sack he plunged down the steps and swung by the clothesline, snatching off his shirt and shot-up britches as he ran by, and then made a beeline for the road.

Ma went back into the house. Pa stood on, where he'd been while all this was going on, for about a minute. Then he caught hold of the milk can and dragged it to the edge of the porch, where he turned it over and poured out what little of the whiskey was left.

"Damn fool idea, anyway," he muttered to himself.

Thunderbolts from Sinai

Uncle Eef didn't show his face around our house for a long time after Ma run him off in July with Pa's double-barreled twelve-gauge shotgun. Then one day about the middle of October he came walking in with his burlap sack and a load of limbs he'd picked up along the road. I saw he had on the britches Ma shot. Somebody had mended them with red-checked calico.

Ma spoke to him as politely as if nothing had ever happened. It was the day the squirrel hunting season opened, and Pa, with our dog Reuben, was just leaving for Mulberry Creek swamp. Pa and Uncle Eef exchanged greetings.

"I'm glad you've come, Eef," Pa said. "Elvira Sudsberry asked if I'd carry her and Julie to church over at Gobbler's Knob tonight. Some wingdinger's gonna preach, and they want to go. Do you think you can hitch old Oliver up to the one-horse wagon and take 'em? I won't get back from squirrel hunting, I'm afraid."

"Certainly, Homer," Uncle Eef said. "You couldn't place them in better hands, and no doubt a little preaching will edify my own soul."

Pa laughed. "Well, just be careful," he said. "Old Oliver could almost go and come by himself, unless something spooks him."

"Have no fear, Homer. I can handle Oliver and ten more like him."

The weather was already chilling, and Ma told me and Mary Lee to bring in some firewood while she milked the cows. Before we had finished, we saw Mis' Elvira coming along a footpath that crossed the big field back of our house.

She was not a big woman, but she had a big bosom and a big low-slung bottom that swung from side to side as she walked, and big feet that splayed out instead of in. She wore her long black gray-sprinkled hair pinned on top of her head in a big ball. There was a wart on her chin with three stiff whiskers sticking out of it. Usually she carried a Bible under one arm, and she always had a vinegary look on her face. She was at our house one day right after Mary Lee learned to whistle. Mary Lee was whistling away, and Mis' Elvira shamed her for it like she'd said a bad cuss word or worse. She said it was a sin for a woman to whistle. Mary Lee wasn't a woman, she was a little girl! But it was a long time before she whistled again. Once when Pa was drunk, he called Mis' Elvira the last crabapple on the butterbean vine.

Ma came across the yard with the milk bucket in her hand as Mis' Elvira opened our back gate. They spoke and came on in the house.

"Where's Mister Foster?" Mis' Elvira asked, darting glances all around the kitchen, blinking her eyes rapidly. "It's near time to go. I don't wanta be late. They've said that Brother Pirkle can preach down the thunderbolts from Sinai. That's what we need to blast the sinners from the back of the house. Where's Homer? Is he ready?"

"Homer's gone squirrel hunting," Ma said, straining up the milk. "Eef's gonna take us."

"Merciful goodness! Do you think we'll be all right with him?"

"Madam," Uncle Eef said, stepping in from the next room where he'd heard what she said. "Why, may I ask, do you question your safety with a man who has driven a wagon train across the Alps? You will be as safe as a butterfly on his mother's breast."

"Oh ... uh ... well, yes, how do you do, Eef?" Mis' Elvira gulped. Then she got hold of herself and said, "Well git the horse hitched up. We've got to git gone from here!"

Uncle Eef gave her a mad look and went out. Mis' Elvira rubbed lots of folks the wrong way with her religion, and she was worse than

Uncle Eef about trying to boss. Mr. Sudsberry wouldn't take her anywhere, and she was always pestering someone to take her to the church services she attended far and near.

"Jesse, you and Mary Lee get ready," Ma said. "You'uns will go to sleep before the service breaks I guess, but I can't leave you here by yourselves. It'll be way after dark fore your Pa gets back."

We got ready, tickled to get to go, though we knowed Ma wouldn't let us sleep while the preacher preached. We'd never heard this Brother Pirkle before, but there was scant chance he'd be any shorter winded than the rest of them.

After Oliver was hitched up to the one-horse wagon, Uncle Eef, wearing the coat Ma made him out of a tow sack and lined with the good part of a wornout sheet, climbed in and sat down on the springboard seat. Me and Mary Lee got in beside him. Ma and Mis' Elvira sat behind us in the two straight chairs they had brought out and put in the wagon.

Old Oliver went along so smooth and easy that we hardly noticed the bumps and holes in the road. When we passed the Daniels's place, we saw Mr. Daniels out at his woodpile chopping wood. Uncle Eef hallooed at him. "Are you not going to the service at Gobbler's Knob tonight, Will?"

"Naw." Mr. Daniels was a man of few words.

We drove on. Uncle Eef reared back, holding the reins with one hand and his meerschaum pipe with the other. He claimed a sultan gave him the pipe, and you could fairly smell his pride rising with the smoke when he'd put it to his mouth and pull. He only smoked it on what he considered to be special occasions.

We could hear Ma and Mis' Elvira talking in their chairs behind us. The sun had gone down, and we saw the sky flush up to a kind of peach-colored glow for a few minutes. Dark was almost upon us as we passed Mr. Rube Griffin's place. Mr. Rube was going up his front steps with several squirrels in his hands.

"Howdy Eef, Mis' Sudsberry, Mis' Foster," he called out to us, holding the squirrels up to show how many he'd shot. Then he asked, "Ya'll headin' fer Gobbler's Knob?"

"We are," Uncle Eef said. "Are you not going?"

"I got to skin these squirrels," he said. "My wife went. Rudolph took her." Rudolph was his son.

"That old hypocrite's mighty frisky," Mis' Elvira said. "I bet he's got a gallon of moonshine whiskey stashed out in the bushes."

"Whiskey maketh a merry heart," Uncle Eef declared stoutly.

Mis' Elvira snorted.

"And man is head of woman!" He just had to get that in.

Mis' Elvira snorted and hissed and thumped her chair.

There was a moon, and it had already begun to shine when we reached Gobbler's Knob church. The kerosene lamps were lit and burning brightly, and a small fire crackled in the cast-iron heater.

The church was nearly half full of people seated on the wooden benches talking. Me and Mary Lee wanted to sit on the back bench with Uncle Eef, but Ma informed us we were to sit right beside her. Mis' Elvira took a seat on the front bench.

Brother Pirkle arrived in the company of Mr. Arly Moss, who owned the big store where we traded. Any preacher who came into our parts to preach always stayed at the Moss home. Mr. Arly would haul him to whatever church he'd been asked to preach. Pa said he told the preachers what to preach, or maybe it would be more correct to say he told them what not to preach. He didn't allow any talk about hell or money.

Brother Pirkle was a strange looking little fellow with a long scrawny neck and a short red beard that frizzed out around his chin. His head was so small it looked almost like a nub topping off his neck. Big eyes sunk way back in his face put you in mind of a skeleton. But when Mr. Arly introduced him, his manner seemed even stranger than his looks.

"How do ye do?" he'd pipe and shake hands with short jerking movements. Then he'd smile a wide possum grin, flashing a passel of gold teeth, and suddenly cut it off as if he didn't know the meaning of a smile; off and on, off and on.

Me and Mary Lee nearly choked trying to keep from laughing. Ma gave us a look that helped sober our faces.

While this introducing was going on, Hop Hawkins and Jake Tankersly arrived with Mae Doll Dooley. Mae Doll was Hop's girl. Folks said she was wild, and I guess she was. Her pa had died, and she done as she pleased and never listened to her ma at all. She always wore bright-red rouge in a perfect circle on each cheek. Hop had been married, but his wife left him. Hop and Jake came in laughing, with Mae Doll, in a short tight dress, between the two men, and all three sat down in the back across from Uncle Eef. More than likely Hop had a jug of whiskey out in his car that he had brought to deliver to some man there in the church.

Mr. Arly raised a hand to them, but the rest of the men kept straight polite faces. All the women's mouths turned down at the corner. Mis' Elvira snorted.

As soon as they were seated, Mae Doll reached over and got a cigarette out of the pack of ready rolls in Hop's breast pocket and stuck it in her mouth. Jake quickly took it out and said something in an undertone. Mae Doll hit at him playfully and laughed.

Aunt Piety, who is Pa's sister, was there with her husband, Uncle Coke, and I heard Aunt Piety say to Ma, "They're all drinking."

Ma nodded her head and said, "I'm afraid so."

Mis' Verdie Griffin went to the organ. Mr. Arly got a hymnbook and said, "Let's turn to page 98." Mis' Verdie began pumping to give us a few notes, and then we all lifted our voices on "I'll Fly Away." I could hear Hop's bass voice above all the others.

When we finished singing the hymn, Brother Pirkle stepped to the platform.

"Brethern!" he shrieked and fell silent. He stood speechless, leaning forward to glare at the congregation so long some began to fidget. Mae Doll giggled a short quick giggle. The only other noise, besides the crackling of the fire in the heater, was a low steady stream of amens coming from Mis' Elvira on the front bench. Mr. Arly, seated on the platform, facing the congregation, looked badly troubled.

"...and Sister-en!" Brother Pirkle finally resumed, jerking himself upright, whamming the rostrum with his fist. "Where did Cain get his wife?"

Folding his arms across his chest, he went stomping around the platform several times. Then he stopped and threw one arm in a long point toward the congregation and yelled, "Babylon is fallen! Woe be unto the profligate and the penny-pinchers!"

All at once Mis' Elvira shot straight up, flung her arms above her head and screamed. Then she crumpled up on the bench.

Ma rushed to her, along with two other women. She sat up. Her eyes had a wild glitter. "Thunderbolts from Sinai!" she cackled, "thunderbolts from Sinai! Preach 'em down, Brother Pirkle, and rid us of the hypocrites in the back of the house!"

I heard a noise behind us and turned to see Uncle Eef going out the back door. The red-calico patch on his britches flashed like a rebel flag. Hop had a sort of mournful look on his face, and Mae Doll looked disturbed, but Jake's jaw was set like steel. When I looked back toward the front of the house, Mr. Arly was crossing and uncrossing his legs rapidly.

Brother Pirkle bent himself nearly double and peered out fiercely. Then he asked in a keen voice of doom, "Where was Moses when the light went out?" He straightened up, sucked in his breath and popped his knuckles. "Ah ... a ... a ... ah," he howled, shaking his head like a dog killing a snake, "Frying on the faggots! Frying on the faggots!"

I think Mr. Arly was right then ready to put a stop to Brother Pirkle when Mis' Elvira rose to her feet shouting. Some man in the congregation hollered amen, and another man echoed it.

Standing on his tiptoes Brother Pirkle made a loud sniffing noise. "Smoke!" he bellowed. "Pile on the hypocrites, Lord, pile on the hypocrites! There'll be gnashing and wailing of teeth!" He ran over and kicked a chair off the platform.

Mis' Elvira kept shouting and clapping. She'd shook all the pins out of her hair, and she was flinging it backward and forward and over and around. Mis' Verdie Griffin broke out with a few shouts. Amens were popping out in the congregation like popcorn on a hot stove. Somebody started singing "Swing Low, Sweet Chariot" and others joined in.

Mr. Arly tried to protest then, but it was too late. The congregation was stirred up, at least part of it was. I saw Ma and Aunt Piety look at each other anxiously.

The next think I knowed Mis' Elvira ran down the aisle till she reached Hop Hawkins and began beating him over the head with a hymnbook. "Git up from thar, you reprobate," she bleated, "and git in that mourner's bench!"

Hop ducked his head and dodged around under Mis' Elvira's attack. I guess he didn't know what else to do, so he got to his feet. Mis' Elvira began beating him in the back with her fists, shouting, "Thunderbolts from Sinai! Even the scum can come!"

Hop moved toward the mourner's bench looking bewildered.

Several other women rushed in and began beating on him. He went down on his knees before the mourner's bench groaning, the women thought it was with repentance, but I think it was from the onslaught of fists.

All this time Brother Pirkle was prancing around the platform with his face blood red, yelping, "Fry the grease outen him, Lord! Fry the grease outen him! Fry him dry!"

Two women had gone back and grabbed Mae Doll by the arms and came pulling her up the aisle between them. The rouge stood out on her cheeks like two headlights. She was scared all right and mad, too, 'cause she tried to jerk loose.

"Turn me loose, you damn fools!" she screamed. "Ow! Stop that pinching my butt!"

Grim faced, they brought her to the mourner's bench and pushed her down beside Hop. The smell of Blue Waltz perfume and corn whiskey reeked in the air. One of the women would yell, "Hold on!" and another would cry, "Let go!"

I glanced over at a window and saw Uncle Eef looking in. He caught me looking and began to motion wildly. I punched Ma, and when Uncle Eef got her eye, he made signs for us to get out of there. Ma looked stunned. I guess she knowed there was no way she could get Mis' Elvira out at that time.

"Remember Potiphar's wife!" Brother Pirkle brayed and smote the rostrum with first one fist and then the other. Then after a pause, he shouted, "Somebody take up a collection!"

Mr. Arly let out a roar that topped any noise we'd heard that night and made for Brother Pirkle. Brother Pirkle eluded him and bolted for the door. Jake Tankersly grabbed furiously for him as he went by, but Brother Pirkle dodged and escaped into the night.

By that time Hop and Mae Doll had broke free from the mourner's bench and were making for the door. "Let's go!" Jake barked, and they went.

Suddenly there was Uncle Eef at Ma's elbow. "Gather your offspring, Mis' Foster," he said, "and I'll fetch Mis' Sudsberry." As we started out I heard him saying, "Unless you wish to be left high and dry, madam, you'd better hit for the wagon."

We made it to the wagon and got in. Uncle Eef lifted the lines, and Oliver started off. The moonlight was so bright I could see people still coming out the church door. Some was milling around in the yard, and some was getting into their wagons and cars. Oliver began trotting as we left the church grounds.

I looked back just as Mis' Elvira stood up and did a few claps with her hands, and I knowed she still had some shouting left in her. But at that moment I heard a noise as something stirred in the back of the wagon. Mis' Elvira heard, too, and turned around, and an unearthly shriek broke from her as a dark figure rose up back there. I saw it was Brother Pirkle.

"What in damnation's wrong with you, madam?" Uncle Eef hollered as Oliver reared up, snorting and nickering, pawing the air with his front feet. When he came down, he left Gobbler's Knob like a homesick bullet.

Me and Mary Lee somersaulted over the back of the seat and landed in a sprawl on the floor of the wagon bed. Ma's chair turned over, and she came down beside us. Mis' Elvira, who was still standing, went staggering forward. The wagon lurched as it hit a hole, and she came reeling backward, stepping on us, till she struck the wagon seat and went down to her knees. She twisted and got hold of the back of the seat and hung there blabbering, "Thar's a haint in this wagon, thar's a haint in this wagon," over and over. Her long hair was streaming straight out behind her head. She had failed to recognize Brother Pirkle.

Brother Pirkle got up to a hunkering position and shrieked, "Sister! Sister! I ain't no haint, but I soon will be lessen somebody stops this wagon! Stop this wagon, you heathen!"

Mis' Elvira couldn't hear him above her screams, and neither could Uncle Eef. He had his feet braced against the front of the wagon bed shouting, "Whoa! Whoa, you inverted fool! Halt and desist! Whoa, I say!" But Oliver paid him no mind. He kept right on busting the wind, while Mis' Elvira's screams went from one pitch to another. As we went flashing past Rube Griffin's place, his dogs took out after us as if we were the mortal enemies. They chased us about half a mile, snapping and snarling and barking. Oliver seemed to go faster, though I doubt that was possible. Right in the middle of the racket, I looked up and saw Brother Pirkle getting to his feet. The next instant he went over the side of the wagon hollering, "My body and soul's a partin'!"

We left him behind, and the next thing I knowed Mis' Elvira's screams stopped, and she slid down on the floor of the wagon.

"She's fainted!" Ma yelled. "What can I do?"

"Leave her alone, madam!" Uncle Eef called back. "For God's sake don't wake her up!"

With Brother Pirkle gone and Mis' Elvira quieted, Uncle Eef got Oliver slowed down to a normal speed. Ma was sitting up now on the floor of the wagon with Mis' Elvira's head in her lap. In a few minutes Mis' Elvira came to and sat up.

"Where's that haint?" she began to jabber. "Where's that haint! Where is it?"

"There wasn't no haint, Elvira," Ma said. "That was Brother Pirkle."

"Brother Pirkle?" she hollered. "How come him in this wagon? Where is he now?"

"He jumped out," I said before Ma could answer.

That was the first Uncle Eef knowed about Brother Pirkle having been in the wagon. It made him so mad that he called Brother Pirkle a jaybird. "That confernal jaybird hid out in this wagon to evade the clutches of Arly Moss! He pert near got us kilt. I'd throwed him out iffen he hadn't already jumped out!"

Pa came out to meet us when we got home. He opened the gate to let us in the barnyard.

"Well, how did the meetin' go?" he inquired jovially. Then he saw Ma and Mis' Elvira sitting on the floor of the wagon bed, and he said, "Why Julie, are you all right? What happened?"

Uncle Eef spoke up before Ma could say a word. "It's a miracle from the Almighty we ain't all quartered and drawn, Homer. That feller Pirkle is devoider of sense than a piss ant! He got them folks waxed up to a frenzy, and then when Arly went for him, he ducked out. Jaybird hid out in our wagon and frighted Mis' Sudsberry into a fit, and Oliver run away!"

Pa laughed as he helped Ma and Mis' Sudsberry out of the wagon. "I thought you said you could handle old Oliver and ten more like him, Eef."

"It little behooves you to laugh, Homer. Neither Lucifer nor Michael the Archangel could handle Oliver or any other horse with Elvira Sudsberry screeching in his ear. Pirkle jumped out of the wagon and she fainted was all that saved us."

"I saw you gawkin' through a window tonight, Eef Kinnard!" Mis' Sudsberry suddenly bristled. "Them thunderbolts from Sinai was too much fer you, wadn't they, you old reprobate?"

"Don't ever ask me to take that woman to church again!" Uncle Eef stormed out.

The Courting of Uncle Eef

We were at the supper table when the scream reached our ears.

"That's Elvira," Ma said.

"That's Elvira, all right," Pa agreed. "Nimroe must be worse. I better get over there."

Ma got up from the table. "I'll come with you," she said.

"Jesse, you and Mary Lee stay here with Eef," Pa was saying when Uncle Eef, who had that day arrived at our house for one of his visits, cut Pa short.

"Homer, I am surprised at you. Have you not yet discerned my talent for consolation in times of tribulation? If Nimroe is dying or dead, Elvira needs my balm of Gilead."

"All right, suit yourself," Pa snapped as he went out the door running, with Ma following.

"Can we go too?" Mary Lee called out.

"No. You and Jesse stay here," Ma called back.

Mary Lee flopped back down at the table, crying. I felt like crying, but I didn't. It wasn't fair. Uncle Eef could go but not us.

Mr. Sudsberry had been ailing for months. He had emphysema, then took pneumonia. Mis' Elvira, his wife, had her hands full taking care of him. That's what I heard Ma say.

It was April. We could hear the whippoorwills in the woods on every side. We could also hear some loud squalling coming from the direction of the Sudsberrys'.

After about an hour Ma came back. "Mr. Sudsberry is dead," she said. "Pa went to get Dr. Tumsen, but Mr. Sudsberry died before they got back. Eef insisted on staying right there with Elvira until others got there, and Pa is staying too. I'm going back."

So we buried Mr. Sudsberry about the middle of April. At the funeral we made a discovery. We discovered that Uncle Eef's "balm of Gilead" had overshot the mark. It had struck a romantic chord somewhere in Mis' Elvira, causing her to take a shine to Uncle Eef.

She fainted at the graveside and fell right into Uncle Eef's arms. He was standing by ready to give out more "balm of Gilead," but when she actually lay in his arms anyone not knowing better would have thought a mad dog had fallen back on him.

Some women took over Mis' Elvira, and Uncle Eef left that graveyard. He was not running, but he was walking as fast as it would be possible to walk and not be running. His face, the glimpse I got of it, was dark and lowering. He had on the green-checked britches and the yellow-dotted shirt that Ma found in the bargain basement at Whithalls and bought for his birthday. The britches were too big, as were all his britches. He was a small man, and the legs were flapping a tune.

I caught a gleam in Pa's eyes that came and went in a flash. Then the funeral moved on to its somber close.

When we arrived home after the funeral, we found Uncle Eef sitting before a small fire he had built to break the evening chill. The burlap sack that he used to carry all his belongings in was setting beside him, packed to go.

"Why, Eef," Pa said, "you're not going to leave now are you? You only got here yesterday." Eef normally stayed a week or two before moving on to another family.

"Homer," Uncle Eef said, his voice quivering with indignation, "you saw what that woman done. She fell into my arms like a bride into the arms of her bridegroom. Little did I imagine that my offers of comfort would or possibly could have such an effect on Elvira. I must flee this place and I may never get to darken your door again. From henceforth I may be a wanderer and a vagabond, a stranger in a strange land."

"Heck amighty, Eef!" Pa broke in, "you're just jumping to conclusions. You know Elvira doesn't like you one bit more than you like her. She was just off guard, feeling a little soft. After all, you did spread some right sticky comfort on her. But that won't last a nickel's worth."

"Alas, I did get carried away," Uncle Eef admitted with a sigh. "I must remember to exercise care ever after in such matters. Then, Homer, it is your opinion that Elvira won't kick over the traces any more?"

"That's right, Eef. I don't think you have thing to worry about."

But Pa was mistaken.

Mis' Elvira come over to our house the next afternoon for a brief visit. She had on her gray taffeta dressy dress. She was a big-bosomed woman with a broad coarse face. There was no way she could make herself dainty and tempting, but she must have had on half a box of talcum powder. Seemed like she had a halo of smell-good surrounding her whole body.

She visited with Ma a few minutes and then went through the house to the front porch where Uncle Eef was sitting in the swing.

He didn't even know she was on the place until she pushed the screen door open and stepped through. His eyes bugged out, and he turned stiff as a poker. Flight was written all over him.

"Good afternoon, Mr. Kinnard," Mis' Elvira said in a dovelike voice. "How are you?"

"I'm in fine fettle, madam," Uncle Eef said. He sounded like a man who was rolling up his sleeves to fight. He got to his feet.

"Sit back down, Mr. Eef," Mis' Elvira cooed. "I come over here to ask your advice."

"About what, Madam?" He eased back down in the swing.

"About a car. I'm going to buy me a car." She took a seat in a chair, having better judgment than to risk getting in the swing. "I know very little about cars. I tried to get Nimroe to buy one, but he wouldn't even talk about it. I feel sure you can tell me the kind to buy."

Uncle Eef knew no more about cars than Pa's bird dog, but Mis' Elvira had hit a live vein. Uncle Eef was crazy about cars, and he doted on giving advice, especially if someone asked for it. It puffed him up until sometimes he would lose the ability to rightly judge a matter.

They sat there (Mis' Elvira had moved into the swing) and engaged in a low sociable conversation for some time. When Mis' Elvira got up to go home, Uncle Eef had agreed to go with her to town the next day to help her pick out a car. They would catch a ride with Mr. Vester Logan, who always went to town on Saturday.

At the supper table that night Pa said, "Looked like Elvira was all spruced up this afternoon when she come where I was working on my harrow. Did she come on any business?"

Silence.

Pa looked all around the table. He laughed an awkward little laugh.

"Elvira is going to buy a car," Uncle Eef said with vast importance. "And she had the good sense to request my help in choosing the kind to buy."

"Oh-o-oh," Pa said, looking at the ceiling. I knew he was all blown up with laughter. "You're going with her to give her the advantage of your knowledge of cars?"

"I am! And you can get that smirk off your face, Homer. The woman needs my excellent advice, and it behooves me to help her. I would appreciate it eternally if you'd keep your jokes to yourself."

"Okay, Eef, you got it," Pa said and got on with his supper.

The next morning Uncle Eef put on his green-checked britches and yellow-dotted shirt, combed his thistledown hair and sat on the front porch to wait for Mis' Elvira. Mary Lee and me joined him, although we knew he had rather we went on and played. The birds and the bees and the butterflies were crisscrossing the yard and fields. The scent of freshly turned earth was on the air.

Mis' Elvira arrived dressed again in her gray taffeta with her pocketbook clutched tightly under her arm. Mr. Vester Logan drove up and stopped. Uncle Eef and Mis' Elvira got in the car, and they drove off.

"I wanted to go to town with Mis' Elvira and Uncle Eef," I grumbled, "but Pa wouldn't let me. I know ten times more about cars than them two put together."

"Huh!" Mary Lee sniffed. "Who's gonna drive it back if she buys one? I sure wouldn't ride in any car one of them was driving!"

It was past the middle of the afternoon when we heard a loud popping noise coming from down the road. Naturally we ran out swiftly to see what it was. It was a car, a sickly tan-colored car, tall, thin, and rickety. As we stared, the car belched and lurched, and about then we recognized Uncle Eef and Mis' Elvira in the front seat, with Uncle Eef driving.

He was twisting the steering wheel so that the car zigzagged back and forth across the road as it came. His face was grim, and so was Mis' Elvira's. Reaching our mailbox, Uncle Eef drove straight into the post and knocked it down. The car then popped like a rifle shot and went dead. We dashed out to investigate.

"Why, Mr. Eef," Mis' Elvira was saying, a little crossly but yet with patience, as we reached the car. "That's the third mailbox you've knocked down today."

"Madam!" Uncle Eef snorted. "This is the most difficult vehicle I ever navigated. It hardly resembles the powerful limousines I'm used to driving." He was dripping wet with sweat, his face was red as a ripe cherry, and he was trembling violently. "Maybe you just better drive it yourself!"

"Oh no, no, no!" Mis' Elvira protested. "I'm not criticizing you, Mr. Eef. You just go in the house and lie down. We'll leave the car right here. Homer can move it himself if he wants it out of the way when he puts the mailbox back up. I'm going home and bake you an egg custard."

Uncle Eef lost no time getting in the house, and Mis' Elvira left. I immediately began investigating that car. It had no back seat. There was a pile of hay where the seat should have been. Getting into the front seat, under the steering wheel, I took hold of it, and pretended I was driving. I knew I could drive it (Pa was beginning to teach me), but I knew I better not. The seat cover was frayed and ragged. How much, I wondered, did Mis' Elvira pay for that car?

Uncle Eef ate very little supper. He had eaten the whole egg custard when Mis' Elvira brought it without offering anyone else a bite.

"Well, I see you knocked down the mailbox," Pa said right away.

"Is that all you've got to say, Homer?" Uncle Eef said somewhat huffily.

"I could think of some other things," Pa said. "Like, I see Elvira has got her hooks in you."

"She has not!" Uncle Eef snapped. "It fairly rattles my soul to see you are so lacking in finesse, Homer! I merely helped the woman choose a car and drove it home for her."

"And ate her egg custard," Pa said.

"It would have been exceedingly rude had I refused the custard. She only wanted to show her appreciation for my help."

A few minutes passed as we ate, and then Pa said, "Why don't you marry her, Eef? You'd have a home and someone to keep you company."

"Damnation!" Uncle Eef shouted, leaping up from the table, turning his chair over, yelling as he went out the door. "I don't need anybody to keep me company, Homer Foster!" He went through the house to the front porch. When he was gone Ma spoke.

"Poor Elvira. I do believe she has really set her cap for Eef. She doesn't know she has no chance whatever of getting him."

"Poor Elvira, my foot!" Pa sniffed. "Whatever got into her to try to spark Eef, the way she has always despised him? Has she gone crazy?"

"No, Homer," Ma said. "Elvira is one of those women who think it is absolutely necessary for a woman to have a husband. She'd marry him, and treat him like she did Nimroe. Of course she didn't make much off of Nimroe, if you remember."

"Yes, and she'd make less off of Eef. He's a crusty old codger, but I'd hate to see him get a bum deal and get beat down in his old age. On the other hand though, I'd hate to see him commit murder."

"Don't worry," Ma said. "Elvira will never lead Eef to the altar."

"I guess not."

The next day was Sunday. Uncle Eef ate a quick breakfast and disappeared in the direction of the barn. When I followed him after I'd finished my breakfast he was nowhere to be seen. I heard a noise in the barn loft.

"Uncle Eef?"

"Shut your infernal trap, Jesse," he said barely loud enough for me to hear him. "Get back to that house, and don't you dare tell that woman where I am!"

I went back to the house. It was Decoration Day at church, and Ma was buzzing around getting ready to go. Pa had agreed to go with her that day, and he was shining his shoes. Mis' Elvira arrived long before time to leave for church.

"Where's Mr. Eef?" she asked.

"I don't know," I lied. "He's around here somewhere I guess."

She went out to her car and began looking it over. She got in under the steering wheel. "Can you drive, Jesse?" she asked.

"Yes, ma'am, some. Pa lets me drive a little." My heart leaped. But she didn't want me to drive. She wanted me to show her how to drive.

I gave her all the instructions I knew and refused her invitation to join her for a drive. Of course, it fell to me to crank the car. It took a long time, but when it finally sparked it lurched forward, missing me by a hair's breadth, and struck out across Pa's freshly ploughed field like it was something alive, popping wildly. I could hear Mis' Elvira's screams above the car noise. Then it went dead.

Hearing some loud hollering, I looked around to see Uncle Eef hightailing it from the barn. "Stop! Stop! Stop that car you infernal air-headed female!" he screeched. "You are going to annihilate it, you spider-brained ...." He passed me with the liveliness of a young rooster, speeding on across the ploughed ground. I followed.

I guess Uncle Eef was primed with every reproach and uncomplimentary word in his system, but when he reached the car Mis' Elvira was weeping as hard as a body can weep. Of course this was the one thing that could have stopped Uncle Eef.

"Don't cry, Madam," he said. "The world hasn't come to an end yet. I guess maybe the vehicle isn't completely ruined! But," and he spoke a little sharper, "why in the name of tarnation did you try to drive that car? You know you don't know how to drive!"

"I don't know why I did it," Mis' Elvira said between sobs. I didn't put much stock in them sobs. "My heart was crushed over the loss of my Nimroe, I guess I just didn't know what I was doing. Oh, boo-hoo!"

This, of course, triggered Uncle Eef's bent toward consolation, and he began trying to stem her flood of grief. She quieted down, wiped her eyes, blew her nose, and said in a pitiful voice, "Will you take me to church, Mr. Eef? I want to put flowers on my Nimroe's grave."

He said he would.

It took every one of us, including Ma and Mis' Elvira, to get the car out of that field. Pa called it a push-mobile.

Pa tried to talk Uncle Eef and Mis' Elvira into riding with us to church, but nothing doing. Uncle Eef informed Pa he could drive anything anywhere. They left ahead of us. Mary Lee and me wanted to ride with them, but we had better sense than to ask.

They were just getting out of Mis' Elvira's car when we drove up. "Why, they should have already gotten here," Ma said. "They left a good while before we did."

"I'm surprised they got here at all," Pa said.

We all went to the cemetery to put flowers on our dead kinfolks' graves. Mis' Elvira acted so downcast and brokenhearted at Mr. Sudsberry's grave, Uncle Eef obliged her when she asked him to go inside with her. He felt, I guess, a measure of safety seeing how broken up Mis' Elvira was over her late husband.

The church house was full. After we sang several songs, the preacher took the pulpit and waded right into his sermon. It was not long until he had thunderbolts from Sinai mixing with fire and brimstone and sinners screaming for the rocks and the mountains to fall on them. I was where I could see Mis' Elvira's face. It began to twitch. Uncle Eef looked to me to be holding his bottom about an inch above the bench.

All at once Mis' Elvira jumped up and began beating Uncle Eef on the back, shouting, "Oh Mr. Eef, you've got to repent! You're hanging over hell like a spider on a web, but I'll never give you up! Give in! Pray through! Turn loose! HOLD ON! I want to be your lawfully wedded wife!"

Before she finished this jibber-jabber, Uncle Eef was gone. He darted out the door like a bird before a rain swell.

Mis' Elvira sat back down. The preacher held his fire a minute, and in that pause we heard the sound of a car just cranked. We knew it was Mis' Elvira's car.

Mis' Elvira came up off that bench like she was electrically wired and left the church house running. We heard her screaming, "Stop! Stop! Stop that car, you thieving scoundrel!" The sound of her voice faded as she went down the road in pursuit of Uncle Eef and her car.

Pa stood to his feet, cleared his throat and said, "Pardon me, Brother Lester, but I think me and my family better go see about them two lovebirds."

"I'm not going, Homer Foster!" Ma whispered indignantly. "You know I've got to be here to put out our dinner at noon!"

"Okay, Julie," Pa answered in low tones. "Jesse, you and Mary Lee come with me. We'll be back for dinner."

A quarter of a mile down the road we overtook them. The car had gone dead on Uncle Eef. Mis' Elvira had caught up with him and was just pulling him out of the car. He had a tight grasp of the steering wheel, but he was no match for Mis' Elvira. As we drove up and stopped, she pried his hand loose, swung him around, and tossed him away from the car. She got under the steering wheel.

"Crank this car, Jesse," she ordered.

"Don't you crank that car for that female goon!" Uncle Eef shouted as he got to his feet. "She'll wreck it!" He lunged at the front door of the car.

"Wait a minute now, Eef," Pa called to him, getting out of our car. "That car belongs to Elvira, remember." Then he turned to Mis' Elvira and said, "You're liable to get hurt, Elvira. Why don't you ...."

"I want Jesse to crank this car," she said.

"Okay, Jesse, crank it."

Uncle Eef was prancing around, making chomping sounds, but Pa kept him back.

I cranked the car after half a dozen attempts. As it cranked, I jumped sideways, and it was a lucky thing I did, for almost instantly it leaped forward. It shot down the road and hadn't gone over fifty yards till it left the road and landed in a ditch.

We raced after the vehicle as Mis' Elvira's screams split the Sunday air. She was out of the car by the time we reached her. The car had gotten the worst end of that stunt. One wheel was twisted and sported a flat tire. The radiator was pushed in. The hood was up.

"I hope you are happy, Madam!" Uncle Eef hollered in Mis' Elvira's face. "You have played havoc with a noteworthy means of conveyance. I hope you are happy!"

"I'm happier than you are, you blasphemous old goat!" Mis' Elvira retorted. "Ruined or not ruined, you'll never drive this car again. I tried to treat you decent, and look what happened!"

I thought for a few moments Uncle Eef was going to pass out with fury. Then he got his voice back. "You hear that, Homer?" he gasped. "Tried to treat me decent! Poof! Tried every trick in the book to lure me into her den so she could marry me!"

"No such thing, you heathen!" Mis' Elvira screeched.

"Here, here now," Pa interrupted. "Let's all get in my car and go back up to the church and devour some of those choice victuals the women will be putting on the table right away. Eef, you and Elvira better shake hands and call it quits."

Uncle Eef shook his head. "No, Homer," he said. "I wouldn't ride in a car with that woman if I knowed it would launch a thousand ships!"

"You better not ride in mine," Mis' Elvira said.

"Ha! No danger of that, Madam," Uncle Eef said. "I doubt anybody will ever ride in that bugger again."

Mis' Elvira started to speak, but he cut her short. "Go on back to the church, Homer. I'll make it back on foot. I'll catch a ride back to your house. I will only be there long enough to pack my sack. Then I shall bid you and your family a long farewell."

"Shucks, Eef ...." Pa started to speak.

"Save your breath, Homer. I must put distance between me and that schemer."

"You needn't leave on account of me," Mis' Elvira huffed. "I'll never again darken the door of a house you are in. Never!"

"Jesse, you and Mary Lee get in the back seat and let Elvira ride in the front seat." When we were all in, Pa turned around and drove off. We looked out the back window of the car and saw Uncle Eef trudging along the dusty road shaking his fist at us. Of course we knew he was really shaking it at Mis' Elvira.

Montezuma Stew

Me and Pa and Uncle Eef had been putting nitrate of soda around the corn in the lower bottom and around the watermelons. As soon as we walked into the house, Ma met us with the news.

"Ma's had a stroke," she said. "She's in the hospital in Selma. I got a letter from Viola in today's mail. She thinks I'd better come. Can you take me, Homer?"

"Now just a minute, Julie," Pa said, hanging his hat on the wall. "Don't get carried away. Are you gonna take the kids?"

"Yes." Then she wrung her hands. "Oh, I forgot," she said.

"Forgot what?" Pa asked.

"They've been exposed to the chicken pox. Either one or both of them could break out any time. I can't take them."

"Dad-bog, if that ain't so," Pa said. "Maybe Elvira Sudsberry could see after them till I get back. She'd be willing to milk the cow, I reckon. Jesse and Eef could see after the feeding."

"Elvira's ailing," Ma said. "She sprained her ankle, and she's got the summer stomach complaint."

"Elvira's got the trots, huh?" Pa said.

"What air you two talking about?" Uncle Eef broke into the conversation to demand. "Do you not think I can take care of these two whippersnappers?" he demanded. "I can manage them with my left hand and tend to whatever else needs tending to with my right hand."

"What if they come down with chicken pox?" Ma asked. "Could you manage then?"

"Certainly, Madam, certainly!"

"But what about the cow?" Pa asked. "You can't milk a cow, can you?"

"Homer," Uncle Eef said, "you grieve me with such an idle question. Have I never told you that I once milked a herd of buffalo in Mexico?"

Pa snorted.

"I may have to stay awhile," Ma told us when she got herself ready to leave about the middle of the afternoon. "But your Pa will be back no later than tomorrow afternoon. You young'uns behave."

That's how me and Mary Lee happened to get left in Uncle Eef's care for a day and night. We watched Pa's car till it disappeared around a curve below the house. Then we went back into the house.

Uncle Eef had his meerschaum pipe lit and going. He had tied a knot in each panel of the kitchen curtains and looped them up over nails in the wall on both sides of the windows.

"What in damnation air you staring at?" he asked when he saw us looking at the windows. "I need more light in this kitchen. Your Ma ain't got sense enough to know that!"

"Ma's gonna be mad," I said.

"Let her pop," Uncle Eef said. "Man is head of woman."

He brought out the big iron pot Ma cooks green beans and turnip greens in and set it on the stove. He had the most pleased, excited look about him you can imagine. I had a feeling it boded us no good. He was always wanting to try his hand at cooking, but Ma wouldn't ever let him. Now he had his chance.

"Children," Uncle Eef said, after knocking out his pipe and taking stock all around the kitchen shelves and in the pantry. "How would you like to feast on Montezuma Stew for supper?"

"What's that?" Mary Lee asked.

"You may well ask," Uncle Eef said, looking like a rooster about to crow. "It's a dish an Indian chef in Mexico taught me to make."

"You mean Indian chief," I corrected him.

"I do not!" He snapped. "I mean chef. Air you not familiar with that word, boy? It means a top-notch cooker."

"Oh. Well, you don't need to cook anything. Ma left plenty for our supper."

"There's just one hitch," Uncle Eef went on, not paying a speck of attention to what I'd said. "Some of the ingredients I'll need are not to be found in this kitchen, so we must make a trip to the store."

"When?"

"As soon as I can catch up some chickens to trade for what I need."

"I don't think Ma's got any chickens she wants to get rid of," I objected quickly.

"Your Ma is away, Jesse," he said, "and I'm in charge. Why in damnation do you argue with everything I say?"

I didn't say anything else.

Uncle Eef found some of Pa's fishing line and cut some two-foot-long lengths. We went outside. There was not a cloud in the sky. The sun was beating down hot enough almost to pop corn. The thought of a trip to Mr. Arly Moss's store a mile away at this time of day made me squirm. But there was no use to argue with Uncle Eef.

He got some corn from the crib and shelled it and threw some of it into a big coop. A bunch of chickens crowded in to eat the corn. Uncle Eef slammed down the lid on the coop. Then he opened it just enough to get his arm in, caught a chicken by the leg, and brought it out.

"That's my Tootsie!" Mary Lee screamed. "You turn my Tootsie loose! You can't sell her!" She lit into Uncle Eef tooth and nail.

He let the chicken go. She flew across the yard squawking wildly. The chickens in the coop were scrambling over each other, making every kind of chicken noise imaginable. Uncle Eef cracked the coop lid again and brought out another chicken.

"That's one of Ma's wyandotte pullets!" I yelled in Uncle Eef's ear. "She's gonna keep every one of them wyandottes!"

I knew by the way he tossed the wyandotte into the air he was hoppin' mad. The next chicken he brought out was another wyandotte, but when I started to open my mouth Uncle Eef roared for me to keep quiet, so I did.

He caught five chickens, and three of them were wyan-dottes. Looking too grim to be crossed, he tied their legs together with the fishing line.

"Now, Jesse," he said. "Me and you will tote two chickens each, and Mary Lee can tote one."

"I don't want to tote an old chicken," Mary Lee grumbled. "She'll do something on me."

"Not if you tote her right," said Uncle Eef. He showed her how to hold the chicken crossways in front of her.

Then me and Uncle Eef got two chickens, one under each arm, and we set off. I had a feeling that if Ma could see us taking off with her wyandottes, she'd have Pa leave Selma on two wheels to stop us.

"I'm hot," Mary Lee said before we'd hardly got started.

"Air you not willing to suffer a little for a stew that the Queen of Sheba served in Montezuma's court?" Uncle Eef asked.

"I thought you said it was an Indian chef in Mexico," I said.

"Jesse," he snapped. "A boy who eternally contradicts his elders will end up on a rock pile!" He hunched up his chickens and walked a little faster.

I was glad when we left the road and turned onto the footpath that led through the woods to the store. We'd cut off nearly a quarter of a mile that way. Also the hot sand in the road was burning mine and Mary Lee's feet.

The leafy branches of the oaks and hickories and sweet gums would keep the path in shade most of the way. I heard a dove cooing, and a bobwhite whistled. The green growing smell of the woods mixed in with the sweet scent of the grancy graybeard. I drawed in some deep breaths and thought how I loved it. White-faced bumble-bees and amber-colored honeybees were courting the wildflowers to steal their nectar. (Pa told me that.) If we hadn't been toting chickens, it would have been a happy time.

We walked single file with Uncle Eef in front, me behind, and Mary Lee in the middle. Every now and then she would toss her black curly hair and look back at me with her lips stuck out. I knew she was about to cry. I'd hunch up my chickens and kick a rock or a stick to let her know how mad I was.

We stopped at a little spring about halfway to the store for a drink of water, and the chickens got away from us. I never dreamed chickens could travel so fast with their legs tied together.

"Damnation!" bellowed Uncle Eef, "Ketch them fowls, children!"

So we chased them and caught them and set off again for the store. Mr. Arly was some surprised to see us. I think he was more surprised to see Ma's wyandotte pullets. But I guess the look on Uncle Eef's face forbade him to speak. Instead, he asked me and Mary Lee a question as he took the chickens and put them in a mesh wire coop just outside the store door.

"Where's your Ma and Pa, children?"

"They're gone to Selma," Mary Lee said.

"Grandma Ledbetter had a stroke," I added.

"These children air in my care," Uncle Eef bristled before Mr. Arly could say more. "They require nourishment, and I intend to supply it. Homer and Julie left me without funds, and I'm temporarily broke, so I've brought these chickens to trade with."

"But Eef," Mr. Arly said, "Julie prizes these wyandottes."

Uncle Eef cut him short. "Arly," he said, "could you bear to watch little children suffer to save the feathers of a few mangy chickens?"

Mr. Arly took the chickens. Uncle Eef called for whatever he needed to make Montezuma Stew. He didn't mention the stew to Mr. Arly, but Mr. Arly must have suspected something when Uncle Eef bought a pound of prunes, a can of tripe, half a pound of bologna, a can of pineapple, and a bottle of lemon extract.

As soon as the purchases were sacked, we headed for home. The sun was still high in the west when we got there. Uncle Eef didn't give us a minute to rest.

"Build us a fire in the stove, Jesse," he said. "I'm going to get that stew started."

While I tried to build the fire, Uncle Eef took a jar of Ma's pear preserves from the pantry shelf, opened them, and dumped them into the big iron pot. Then he broke about six eggs into the preserves. After that he added the prunes, the bologna, the tripe, the pineapple, and the lemon extract.

"Ugh! I'm not gonna eat that stuff," Mary Lee announced indignantly.

"I'm not going to eat it, either," I said, throwing down the kindling. "It ain't fit to eat!"

"Why you thankless poppinjays," Uncle Eef said, stirring in half a jar of pepper sauce. "There are multitudes of people in this world who would give their eyeteeth for a bowl of this Montezuma Stew!"

Me and Mary Lee seated ourselves on two kitchen chairs. Uncle Eef snatched up the kindling and finished building the fire in the stove.

"You've just wasted Ma's preserves and eggs and all that other stuff, too," I said.

"Jesse, " Uncle Eef said, "you air the sassiest human being it has ever been my experience to know. If you impudent offspring of Beelzebub don't have the taste to appreciate this toothsome viand, I might as well dump it and leave. You two ingrates can spend the night with Elvira Sudsberry!"

"That's all right, Uncle Eef," I said quickly. Of all things we didn't want, spending the night with Mis' Elvira topped the list.

"We like the stew," Mary Lee said. I could tell she was close to tears.

Lying is bad I know, but sometimes there's no way around it. This was one of them times, I reckon. Uncle Eef glared at us a minute, breathing out suspicion. Then he turned back to the stove and stirred the stew.

Me and Mary Lee just sat there in our chairs feeling like orphans in the first degree. Why did Grandma Ledbetter have to go have a stroke? I noticed the sweet scent of the four-o-clocks growing close to the kitchen door. I heard Rosie, our cow, moo, and I knew she'd come up to be milked. Did Uncle Eef really know how to milk a cow?

The stove was red hot and roaring now. Uncle Eef had crammed a handful of rich pine kindling in with the stove wood. He stood by the stove, wet with sweat, stirring the stew. The old pair of britches somebody had patched with red calico bagged way down behind, and his old sweaty threadbare shirt clung to his bony shoulders. Glancing down I saw his heels through the holes in his turned-over shoes. I began to feel sorta sorry for him.

Then the first scent of Montezuma Stew reached my nose, and all pity left me. Any man who would force two little children to eat something that smelled like that deserved no pity.

Me and Mary Lee looked at each other. I felt a rising panic.

Uncle Eef had stepped back from the stove, fanning himself with a pot holder. The expression on his face had changed. As I watched it went from surprise to anxiety. He stepped to the water bucket and drank a dipperful of water.

"Get a fresh bucket of water, Jesse!" he barked at me.

Grabbing the water bucket, I headed for the well with Mary Lee at my heels. Getting out of that kitchen was one thing I welcomed. I could still smell the stew, but it was less deadly out in the open.

Me and Mary Lee never spoke a word as I drawed up the water. What was there to say? If we defied Uncle Eef, he'd leave and we'd fall into the hands of Mis' Elvira. But could we eat the stew? For one crazy second I half hoped it would kill us to spite Uncle Eef.

When we got back with the water, the scent of the stew was walking around in full control of the kitchen. The ucky odor was swooping and swirling so there was no getting away from it. Nobody on earth could have described it. Uncle Eef looked like a man at bay. I guess it was the pepper sauce that nearly strangled us.

We all went outside. We were all silent. I watched Uncle Eef. I saw his old pluck begin to flow back into him. After awhile he spoke.

"Children," he said, "I now perceive that one of the most vital ingredients of Montezuma Stew is Mexican air. The galoot who gave me the recipe failed to mention that."

"That's just an excuse," I said. "I bet you made up that recipe as you went along."

"Jesse," he said. "You are a true vulture. Let a man make one unavoidable mistake, and you're ready to peck out his internal organs."

"You had no business selling Ma's wyandotte pullets." I thought I might as well rub it in now that I had a chance.

"I shall explain that matter to your excellent mother," he said.

Going back into the kitchen he slapped a lid on the iron pot, got a pot holder, and carried the pot outside. He emptied it into the high weeds back of the smokehouse. Then he scrubbed the pot with sand, rinsed it in the watering trough, and left it outside to dry.

The sun was almost down. Rosie stood at the barnlot mooing.

"It's time to milk," Mary Lee said.

"Jesse," said Uncle Eef, "Go turn that cow into the lot, and let the calf have his supper."

"You're not gonna milk her?"

"Do as I say, you infernal contradictor!" he snapped.

I did as he said.

We went back into the house and ate the food Ma had left for our supper. There was no talk. After supper we sat out on the front porch awhile, watching the lightning bugs and listening to the katydids. Every once in a while I'd hear Uncle Eef sigh. He was worried all right. That big talk of his about man being head of woman didn't count for much when Ma got her dander up. Well, he should have thought of that when he was catching Ma's wyandotte pullets and lugging them to the store to trade with.

Twice during the night I woke up and heard Uncle Eef prowling around the house. He woke us at the crack of day to get up and eat breakfast. We each had a boiled egg with leftover cornbread and coffee. Me and Mary Lee didn't drink coffee, so Uncle Eef poured water in our cups. It was a poor excuse for breakfast. Uncle Eef drank four cups of coffee, one right behind the other. Then he squared his shoulders, lit his pipe, and spoke.

"Children," he said, "I'm going to have to leave you."

"How come?" asked Mary Lee.

"Yeah, how come? You promised Ma and Pa you'd see after us till Pa got back," I reminded him.

"I know I did children, but the truth is I'd forgotten a promise I made to help Dark Fowler pull fodder today."

"But you can't go off and leave us!"

"Yes, Jesse, I can. I must. You two can fend for yourselves till your Pa gets back. Dark Fowler needs help with that fodder pulling, and there's nobody but me to help him."

He went into the front room and came back with his croaker sack. Sometime during the night he had gathered up all his possessions and packed them into the sack. The time of his departure had come.

"You're just leaving on account of selling Ma's wyandotte pullets," I said. I was mad at that man.

"Jesse," he said, drawing himself up, trying to look offended. "I am mortally grieved at your impudence." With that he swung his sack onto his back and went out the kitchen door.

"I bet you didn't even promise to help Mr. Dark pull fodder," I flung at him, wishing Ma was there with Pa's twelve-gauge shotgun to give him a scare.

He went around the corner of the house, heading for the road. Me and Mary Lee hurried through the house to the front porch. Uncle Eef was nearly to the road.

"You come back here and stay with us!" I shouted.

"You come back!" Mary Lee screamed.

But he didn't come back. He didn't even look back. We stood there watching him go. As he reached the curve and was passing out of our sight, I thought of something.

"The corn's not ready for fodder pulling!" I ran down to the road and yelled after him.

He disappeared around the curve.

My Brother Willie

Times was bad. Pa had left us, and we had stopped expecting him back. Ma didn't cry any more. She just said things like, "Laid up and begat you and then left you to starve!" or "Better we was all dead and buried!"

We lived in a little run-down house on Mr. Dark Fowler's place. He said, "Noreena, you and the kids can work these patches around here. Willie's old enough to plow. I'll let him use my mule and plow. Raise a big garden and some corn to feed your chickens and cow."

(We didn't even have a cow before Pa left. Grandpa Butts give us the cow to make up for his good-for-nothing son leaving us, he said.)

Willie was my big brother, the oldest. He was eleven. Ma couldn't do anything with Willie. As soon as Pa got gone, Willie took it on himself to do as he pleased. He'd roam around the countryside, visiting with different families, and then come home sassing Ma and trying to run over the rest of us.

When Ma mentioned plowing to him, he said he'd promised to help Mr. Arly Moss at his store. I doubt Mr. Arly had said a word to him about working. He would hang around the store till some old woman like Mis' Katie Higgins would come along and, feeling sorry for him cause his Pa was gone, buy him a strawberry soda. If some man throwed down an inch-long cigarette butt, Willie stuck a pin in it, and went behind the store and smoked it. I saw him do it when Ma sent me with him to get some flour and lard on credit.

"I'm gonna tell Ma you smoked that cigarette butt," I said.

"That's just like a split-tail gal!" Willie snorted. "Go ahead and tell Ma and see if I care! Ma won't do nothing."

When I told Ma, she stopped rocking Ellie, who was two and the baby, and sighed and said, "Well, Darcie, Willie is set on going to the dogs so there's not much I can do."

"Whup him," Buster advised. He was seven.

"Yah! Yah! Yah!" Willie started hollering. Ma grabbed her switch, but he got away as usual.

Buster was trying to get one of Pa's old socks started unraveling so he could make a ball. I went to help him, and the ball was finished when Willie came back in. He wanted to see the ball, and Buster let him have it. He tossed it up and caught it a few times and then stuck it in his pocket.

"Gimme that ball!" Buster yelled.

"I need a ball," Willie said.

"That's my ball, Willie Butts!"

"It's made outta Pa's sock, so I got as much right to it as you have, spunky-punk."

"You give that ball back to him!" I shouted, taking a swing at Willie with the fire poker. Willie dodged and started laughing in a way to taunt us.

Ma came in and called Willie a wretch and things like that, but he wouldn't give back the ball.

Sometimes Mr. Arly Moss took Willie with him when he went into town for supplies. Mr. Arly paid him, but we never knew how much. Willie spent every penny of it for strawberry soda, chocolate bars, and chewing gum, and then come home with the whole pack of gum in his mouth. With them sharp elbows of his on the table, he would pop the gum and tell us what ignoramuses we was cause we hadn't been to town.

Our hens didn't lay when the weather was cold, but when the first of March come, we started listening out for one of them to cackle the news she'd laid. Our mouths were watering for something besides speckled peas and thickening gravy. The cow Grandpa Butts gave us didn't furnish a quart of milk a day. Ever time Ma milked the cow, she'd call her a wretch, but it did no good. Of course we knowed she'd pick up when the grass started growing.

Me and Buster and Willie were up back of our house one morning, playing in Goblin's Cave, when we heard a hen cackling.

"That hen's laid a egg!" Willie exclaimed. "And I'm gonna have it!" With that he went bounding down the hill toward the house.

Me and Buster struck out after him. We figured the egg was as much ours as his, and we meant to show him so.

Ma had nailed some apple crates up on the back of the smokehouse and put some pine straw in them for nests. Willie beat us there and got the egg. When we reached the house Willie was in the kitchen tellin' Ma he claimed the egg first.

"And you got to cook it for me," he was saying when Buster and me come tearing in.

"No fair!" Buster yelled. "That egg's as much ours as it is his!"

"No such thing you knuckle-butt! I claimed first!"

"Give me that egg, Willie," Ma ordered. "I'll scramble it and divide it."

"Nothing doing!" Willie whooped, leaping out the door. He headed down through the pasture. Ma knowed she couldn't catch him so she didn't try. She told us not to fret, the hen would lay another egg the next day, and we could have it.

"What if Willie gets it?" I asked.

Ma sighed. "Well you'll just have to beat him to it, is all I know to tell you." She sighed again. "I may have to send that boy to the reform school," she said.

About an hour later we saw smoke rising up down in the pasture by the tag alder thicket. Me and Buster hurried down there and found Willie just finishing off the egg. He had built a fire of twigs and dead limbs and boiled the egg in an old tin can.

"I hope you get poisoned," I snapped.

"Ma says me and Darcie get the next egg," Buster informed him.

Willie leaned back and laughed like a hyena, so we knowed it would be nip and tuck as to who got the next egg. Me and Buster screwed up every nerve in our bodies in determination it wouldn't be Willie.

We got up the next morning before sunup and, after gulping a fast breakfast, stationed ourselves under the hen nests in two chairs we brought out. It was a long day. No cackle was heard. About mid-afternoon we came in and ate a plateful of speckled peas.

This kept up for three days. Ma let us stay out of school. Willie had already quit school. Finally on the third day, a hen laid. We didn't know if she was the layer of the first egg or not, but me and Buster got it. As it turned out there was no sweat about it, for Willie had gone off on one of his countryside jaunts.

School let out the last day of March, and the next day, Mr. Dark Fowler brought over his mule and plow. "Here son," he said to Willie, who hadn't spotted him in time to make a getaway. "You plow up these patches today. It's time you all was gettin' ready to plant some things."

Willie just stood there looking sullen.

"Well go ahead, boy. You know how to plow don't you?"

"Naw."

"Hells bells!" Mr. Dark snorted. He grabbed up the plow lines. "Here, I'll show you." And off he went opening a furrow across the patch. When he got back he handed the lines to Willie and said, "Here now, lemme see you do that."

Willie turned a furrow nearly as deep and pretty as Mr. Dark's. But I could tell by the look on his face that he was mad and getting madder. Mr. Dark was no sooner out of sight than Willie cut a diagonal furrow to the upper side of the patch and then came zigzagging back.

"I don't aim to plow this danged field!" He shouted and threw down the lines.

"Ma!" I yelled. "Commere quick! Willie don't aim to plow!"

"I swear, Darcie Butts, I'd like to cram a dead cat in yore mouth!" He grabbed a big clod of dirt and sent it hurtling close to my head. Then he sprang over and unfastened the mule from the plow and threw clods of dirt at him. The mule left running.

Ma came tearing out of the house with Ellie on her hip. "Catch that mule!" she shrieked. But the mule was gone, and so was Willie. He had them long legs in action, heading for Goblin's Cave.

When Mr. Dark came for his plow the next day, he never said a word to any of us.

Ma sent me and Buster over to Mis' Fowler's one day to borrow a cup of sugar, and she sent Ma a magazine. Willie was looking at it when he saw the ad inviting people to sell Rosebud Salve and get rich. He announced his intention to order the salve and sell it. Knowing Willie as she did, Ma was against the idea. "You sell that salve and don't pay the company, you'll land in jail, young man!"

Willie ordered the salve. In two days he started sitting on our front porch every day watching for the mail carrier. On the fifth day Willie exploded. He blamed our mailman, Mr. Babcock, for the delay. "Sorry old coot! He orter have a car to deliver mail anyway. That old knuckle-butt horse ain't no good!"

"Well he's gonna get a car, and you know it!" I snapped.

We'd been hearing for several months that the rural mail carriers were going to get cars. All of us kids were waiting for the day when Mr. Babcock would come by driving a car instead of his horse and buggy. Willie called us greenhorns. Said we never had seen anything. But we were not fooled. We knowed Willie would bust a gut if his eyes were not the first to be laid on that car when it came by.

The Rosebud Salve arrived. Willie went out and sold a box and came home with a dime.

"Where's the other dime, Willie," Ma asked. "That salve sells for a quarter, and you only get a nickle on each box."

Willie just sat there looking stubborn with the cowlick on top of his head sticking straight up.

"Where's that dime, young man?"

Willie jumped up. "I ain't got it!" he yelled. "I'm gonna make it up on the next box."

But he didn't. When he sold the last box, all he had was a quarter, and he blowed that on a box of vanilla wafers, a chocolate bar, a strawberry soda, and two packs of chewing gum. (Mr. Arly told Ma that's what he bought.) He came home with one pack of gum in his mouth and divided the other pack with us. I guess he thought that was a fitting gesture before leaving us for a long stretch in jail.

He didn't seem much worried though till he began to get threatening letters from the Rosebud Salve Company. When they told him a lawyer would soon be calling on him, Willie lost his nerve. He woke us all up that night babbling. "I don't wanta go! Leave me alone you galoots!" He came tearing out of bed and hit the wall head on. Then he lay there moaning.

"Wake up Willie!" Ma ordered, "and get back in that bed! I told you about spending that Rosebud Salve money, you wretch! You're driving me crazy!"

Willie had regained much of his courage by the next morning, and when Ma mentioned a job to pay off the Rosebud Salve Company, he didn't pay her any attention whatever. He did go out to the woodpile and chop up about half an armload of stove wood out of the planks Ma had pried off Mr. Dark's cotton house and toted home. And he was jumpy. Once he heard a noise and darted behind the house and sent Buster to see what it was.

"Ain't nothin' but the crib door creakin'," Buster reported. "You shore are skittish, Willie. If they take you to jail, I want my ball back, you hear."

"Shut up!" Willie screamed.

We all went in the house to get a drink of water. Willie had the dipper to his mouth when Ma came running in from the yard and said "I hear a car!" We expected this was the lawyer from the salve company.

Willie dropped the dipper and shot out the back door. He disappeared into the woods back of our house. I knowed he meant to make his last stand in Goblin's Cave. It would be hard for a grown man to get to the back of that cave, so I felt that Willie had a chance.

Then I looked out the front door, and there was Mr. Babcock stopped at our mailbox in a brand new car. We all raced out to admire the car and for an instant we forgot Willie. Then Buster said, "Old Willie's gonna be mad cause he wasn't the first to see this car."

"Car," Ellie repeated, "Willie see."

"It's no matter for him," Ma said. "Maybe he'll sell some more Rosebud Salve and spend all the money."

"Ma'am?" Mr. Babcock asked.

"Oh nothing," Ma answered.

Willie stayed gone all afternoon. We got worried and went to hunt him. Only silence greeted us at Goblin's Cave. We yelled and yelled but got no answer. Ma went up to the cave. By then she was full of pity for poor Willie. We all felt kinder toward him.

"Come on out, Willie," Ma called in a pleading voice. "It's all right, honey."

Still no answer. Buster and me had already been back in the cave. Ma sent us in again. It was almost dark in there, but as I stood searching with my eyes I heard a small movement, and there lay Willie in a little shelf-like crevice at the top of the cave, in the very back. None of us had ever before been able to get up there.

"Come down, Willie." I said. "It wasn't a lawyer, it was Mr. Babcock in a new car."

"Yow-e-e-e-e!" Willie's howl bounced around in that cave like a gunshot. He began to struggle. "I'm stuck!" he roared. "Git me down from here!"

Ma managed to get to the back of the cave, and we all pushed and pulled. Willie was wedged in that crevice with his knees drawn up under his chin. He kept bawling that we were hurting him.

"No matter," Ma said. "We've got to get you down. You can't live up here the rest of your life."

At last we freed him. He hobbled outside. We brushed him off and helped him get his legs straightened out. He was skint all over. He blamed Ma for his ordeal. "And I didn't git to see Mr. Babcock's car!" He said it bitterly and started to cry. "You KNOWED I wanted to see that car!"

Ma patted his shoulder. He jumped back like she was a snake. "Leave me alone!" he bellowed. "Why'd you come in there and say you heard a car?"

"Because I did hear a car, you wretch!" Ma said. "How was I to know it was Mr. Babcock and not that lawyer?"

"You jest wanted them knuckle-butts to see Mr. Babcock's car first," Willie accused.

Ma snatched up Ellie and started to the house. "Next time it will be the lawyer, young man, and you jest see if I warn you. You better make some money to pay that Rosebud Salve Company!"

"I AM!" Willie exploded.

But he never did. Every time he'd make a little money, he'd spend it on candy, chewing gum, and strawberry soda. Ma finally sold Pa's crosscut saw and paid the Rosebud Salve Company, to get them threatening letters stopped.

"We don't need that saw nohow," she said. "We might as well all be dead and buried."

The Christmas Shoppers

Thelma and Cobb McNabb got off the city transit bus in front of Jack's at Roebuck Shopping Center, having come to do their Christmas shopping. It was one week until the "Day."

Cobb, who was sixty-eight years old, a little stooped, wrinkled, and perpetually sour, was not in favor of the trip. "No use'n us going down there and getting strung out in that mess of people," he said, when Thelma broached the subject.

It was exactly the same thing he said every Christmas. Even when the children were small, Cobb was immune to the Christmas spirit. But Thelma had never let him get away with it. She had always managed to have Christmas in spite of Cobb's objections.

"We're a going," she said. "You know we've got to get some presents for the kids and the grandkids."

They had two children, a son and a daughter, and three grandchildren. Their son, Henry, had only one child, although he wanted more. Cobb said it was a merciful blessing Henry could have only one child. It cost too much to raise children. Thelma called him an old sore-headed coot and said she certainly wished they had more grandchildren.

"Likely we'll go down thar and get mugged," Cobb said. "Them young'uns don't need no presents. They got too much already. Don't appreciate nothing. What are you gonna buy me for my Christmas present?"

"I don't know. Whatever I buy you will be more'n you buy me. If somebody was to ask me who I thought was the stingiest, crabbiest human being on earth, I'd say you, Cobb McNabb!" said Thelma, ironing away at his black shirt.

It was 10 o'clock when they stepped down off the bus. Cobb took out his watch and looked at it. The weather was unseasonably warm and brooding, with cloud smears in the sky that looked as if some artist had been wiping his brush.

Cobb had on his black shirt and a pair of baggy old gray trousers, a brown suit coat, and a plaid hat. The scowl on his face set his tone. Thelma, her gray hair short and frizzed with a home permanent, was wearing a blue-checked dress, a white sweater, and flat shoes. She set off briskly in the direction of the stores, grasping her purse firmly with both hands. No thief was going to snatch her purse in a surprise move. There was a pinched yet determined air about her. She was glad there was money in her purse, money that she had saved out of her Social Security check for months, glad she didn't have to worm money out of Cobb.

Cobb followed her, staying about a hundred feet behind, with a chew of tobacco in his mouth. Thelma detested this habit, especially when he chewed in public, but she kept quiet because it only made him worse when she voiced her objections.

"Let him chew his tobacco," she thought. "I'm gonna play bingo and watch my soap operas and he can't stop me." Every few minutes she would half turn and look back. He was coming on in his same slow pace, looking sullen and spitting tobacco juice. "I wish he'd spit on someone and they'd call the police," she thought. Then she turned her mind to what she might buy.

She turned in at Watkin's Book Shop to buy the latest *Candlelight* romance. She never missed one, although she did say the sex made her gag. Her daughter, Muriel, suggested she buy other romance books that didn't have so much sex. But Thelma said no, she didn't have any use for people who were forever changing around, so she'd stick with *Candlelight*.

She had put her book on the counter and was turning to go to the back of the shop where the children's books were, intending to buy one for ten-year-old Hattie Ann, when she noticed Cobb passing the book shop without turning his head. She knew he knew she was in the store and paid him no mind.

When she came out of the book shop twenty minutes later, with her book and *Charlotte's Web* for Hattie Ann, she didn't see hide nor hair of Cobb. After glancing carefully up and down the sidewalk and out across the parking lot, she said to herself, "He sees me. He's somewhere looking at me, where I can't see him." She went on toward J. C. Penney.

She was right. Cobb had turned in at the shoe store next door to the book shop. His intention was to station himself so that he would see Thelma when she passed by, without letting her know he was in there. While waiting, a pair of boots on display caught his eye. He picked one up and gave it a looking over. That was one fancy, high-class pair of boots. They excited him. He had always wanted a pair of boots.

After he saw Thelma's head of short, frizzy gray hair go by, he asked a clerk how much the boots cost. One hundred and fifty dollars, the clerk told him. That gave him a jolt, but instead of discouraging him, the high price increased his excitement and whetted his desire to own the boots.

Thelma had no business dragging me out to go Christmas shopping, he thought. She's got all that money in her purse that she's been saving up to buy stuff for them kids, stuff they don't need!

"I wanta try them boots on," he told the clerk. The clerk looked startled. He hesitated. "Mr… " he started to say something.

Cobb cut him off. "I wanta try them boots on," he repeated.

The clerk measured his foot, found his size, and brought the boots out. They fit. Cramming the legs of his trousers into them Cobb stood up and observed himself in a mirror. Snazzy. That was the word that came into his mind. Them boots looked snazzy. Serve Thelma right if I blow my money on boots while she blows hers on Christmas presents. He bought the boots, counting the cash out of his billfold.

"Anybody mug me now won't get no money," he remarked.

The clerk still had an expression of doubt about him, but he smiled and put Cobb's shoes into the box the boots came in. Cobb walked out wearing the boots, with his trouser legs still crammed into them.

Coming out of the store he walked on up to Penney's and went into the place, but saw no trace of Thelma. After searching every department he left, heading on up toward Pizitz.

Thelma, however, was still at Penney's, having gone to the restroom while Cobb was searching for her. While she shopped, buying shirts and ties for her son and son-in-law and robes for their wives, she kept a sharp lookout for Cobb. Where was he? He usually didn't stay out of sight that long. He was probably afraid if he joined her she'd want some money out of him.

Deciding she would finish shopping for the grandchildren elsewhere, she carried her purchases to the service department for free wrapping and bought a large shopping bag. Slipping her purse handle onto her left arm, she took the loaded shopping bag in her left hand and came out of the store, scanning the area for Cobb again. The sky looked as if someone had scattered a basket of dirty cotton balls up there. The sun was shining intermittently. Seeing no sign of Cobb, she turned her steps in the direction of Pizitz, a half-block up the street.

She was beginning to feel tired and peevish. The least Cobb could do would be to carry her packages. She needed a cup of coffee, maybe a cheeseburger. Where was Cobb? Had harm come to him?

At Roma's Restaurant and Pizzeria she turned in and ordered coffee and a cheeseburger. The place was packed, so she had to sit in a back booth facing away from the front. She failed to see Cobb go by, heading back in the direction from which he had come. Having already been to Pizitz, he was beginnning to limp. The boot heels were higher and the toes were sharper than he had thought.

More clouds had moved into the heavens, and an unpleasant little wind was skipping about. Christmas music and songs were pouring from a loudspeaker located somewhere toward the center of the parking lot. "Silent night, holy night..."

"I'm sick and tired of that Silent Night," Cobb muttered. "I wonder where that woman is." He thought of his prediction that they might get mugged. Suppose something like that had happened to Thelma? Well, she wouldn't have anybody to blame but herself.

Then he felt sure Thelma was deep inside some store, spending money, thinking no more about him than if he were her pet rabbit.

Cobb sat down to rest on a bench in front of Penney's. He lifted one foot and then the other to admire his new boots. They were not as comfortable as he would have liked, but he was still overly proud of them.

A Salvation Army worker came along and stationed herself not far from where Cobb was sitting. She began ringing her bell. Cobb gave her a mad look. Those people probably had so much money they had to keep it in several banks. Thelma was always tossing money, sometimes even bills, into their pots. That woman didn't have any more sense about money than a yellow-bellied sapsucker.

When Thelma finished the coffee and cheeseburger, she left Roma's and went on up the sidewalk to Pizitz. On the way she looked at the clouds and felt uneasy again. Her mind was mostly taken up with thoughts of Cobb.

As she came into Pizitz she looked over the store in hopes of spotting him. Near the escalator she saw a security officer standing. Switching her purse and shopping bag again she approached the officer and explained that she was looking for her husband.

"Did he have on boots?"

"No, sir."

"Huh. Man with boots on came by a little while ago and said he was looking for his wife."

Thelma took the escalator up to the second floor and walked around searching for Cobb. She got a porter to see if he was in the men's restroom.

Passing a table where mechanical toys were being demonstrated by a pretty young woman, she paused. The young woman picked up a fuzzy lifelike dog and wound it. When she sat it back on the table it jumped into the air, turned a somersault, and landed on its feet.

Thelma decided to buy the dog for Cobb's Christmas present. That was more than he'd buy her. He would pretend he didn't like it, but she knew what Cobb liked. He was a simple man.

As soon as she paid for the dog, she put it in her shopping bag and hurried to the escalator to go back down. Coming out of the store she looked around for Cobb again, casting her eyes in every direction. She decided to retrace her steps all the way to Jack's, where they had gotten off the bus. Fatigue was dogging her. She kept changing her purse and the shopping bag back and forth.

At the bench in front of Penney's she put two dollars in the Salvation Army pot and sat down to rest. A black woman wearing heady perfume sat down beside her. She thought about a time, long years ago, when Cobb had bought her a bottle of Blue Waltz perfume. Oh Cobb, where are you?

She rose hurriedly and resumed her walking. She was passing the shoe store where Cobb bought his boots when she spied a man, seated on the curb of the sidewalk in front of Eckerd drug store, bent over and busy at something. The man had on a plaid hat. Thelma's pulse quickened and so did her steps, her eyes riveted on the curb-sitter. It was Cobb. He was changing the boots for his old comfortable shoes.

"Cobb McNabb!" Thelma exclaimed. "Where have you been and what are you doing?"

"I'm gettin' out of these plague-taked boots," he said.

"I've been hunting you! Where in the devil have you been? And where'd you get them boots?"

"I bought 'em!" he said and stuck out his chin stubbornly.

"Bought 'em! How come?" She reached down and got the boot he had pulled off. "Look at them heels and those sharp toes! Cobb, you know you can't wear any such shoes!"

"Well, it's your fault I bought 'em! Dragging me off down here and then running off and leaving me! I'm taking 'em back."

"You can't take them back now, you know that. You've just thrown your money away. How much did they cost?"

"Fifty dollars."

"Fifty dollars! Have you gone crazy, Cobb?"

"No, Thelma, I ain't gone crazy. While you was flinging your money away for Christmas presents I spent mine for boots."

"That you can't wear!"

"Oh I can wear them. I wore them all the way to Pizitz and back."

"So!" Thelma said. "You were the man with the boots on who was looking for his wife!"

Cobb ignored the last shaft. He tied the laces of his old shoes. "It's a pretty come-off," he said. "Man goes shopping with his wife and she takes off like a jenny in heat, looking for a jackass, so's he can't keep up with her and then he gets lost and can't find her!"

"You could'a kept up with me. You more'n likely hid to get me rattled, and your cute little trick backfired."

Cobb snorted.

"I'm gonna take them boots back," he announced. "That man had no business selling them boots to me! He orta knowed a man my age couldn't wear any such shoes."

"Boots, Cobb," Thelma corrected him. "Them's boots, not shoes."

He ignored that shot, too. "You go on and finish your shopping," he said, picking up the box with the shoes in it, "while I tend to this. Where you planning to shop next?"

"I'm going with you," she said.

The last thing on earth Cobb wanted was for Thelma to go with him to the shoe store for a refund and learn how much he had actually paid for the boots. He hesitated, searching for an excuse to get rid of her.

Thelma suspected Cobb had not told her the whole truth about the boots transaction, so she decided to trick him. "O.K.," she said, "I'm going back to Penney's," and set off. Halfway there she stopped and looked back, intending to wave if Cobb was still at the curb. He wasn't. She caught a glimpse of him going in the door of the shoe store. Waiting about two minutes, she changed direction and went back to the shoe store.

As she entered the store she heard two men arguing and one of them was Cobb.

"That's right!" Cobb was saying. "You orta knowed a man my age couldn't wear them needle-toed, spike-heeled boots!"

"I'll admit the thought did cross my mind," the clerk said. "In fact, if you remember, I tried to point out...."

"You didn't try to point out nothing," Cobb informed him. "These doosies are not worth any hundred and fifty dollars."

A strangling noise escaped Thelma. She felt as if her eyeballs were out on stems.

The clerk broke off speaking to Cobb and rushed to Thelma.

"Lady!" he cried. "What's wrong?" He pushed her to a sitting position on a stool.

Thelma gasped but couldn't make a word come out. She pointed toward the boots.

"That's my wife," Cobb said, without moving a peg. "Leave her alone. She was intending to buy these boots for my Christmas present, and she's upset because I went ahead and bought 'em for myself."

At that moment a bolt of forked lightning split the heavens and every light in Roebuck Shopping Center went out. Thelma felt sure the Almighty had spoken.

Jake Raven and Brother Tutt

I could hardly ever tell when Jake was serious and when he was fooling. When he came limping in with the sole of one shoe half torn off and the left leg of his overalls split open from the ankle to the hip, I asked him what happened. He said he'd been raped and then robbed. Of course I suspected him of lying right away when he said he had been raped.

Brother Tutt didn't. (Suspect him of lying, I mean.)

"Tutt, tutt," he clucked, coming through from the mission chapel where the 10 a.m. services were just concluding, to the front foyer where I had let Jake in, in answer to the doorbell. "You better get upstairs and lie down, Jake," he said, "while I call the doctor. Sam," he instructed me, "you assist Jake upstairs while I phone Dr. Smitt."

I shot a look at Jake. He grinned sheepishly. "Hold it, Brother Tutt," he said. "I don't need no doctor."

"Like hay, you don't!" Brother Tutt bristled. (His name was Holyfield but we all called him Brother Tutt because of the expression he constantly used.) "You been raped, you need a doctor."

"Ah, knock it off, Brother Tutt," Jake groused. "I ain't been raped. I ain't even been robbed. How could I be robbed, me without a dumb penny. I had a fight with a grizzly bear."

"Tutt, tutt," the preacher scolded, "I wish you'd stick with the way it is, Jake! You're going to have to give account for every idle word, you know."

I heard Hawkins snigger. He had come from the kitchen to announce the noon meal and overheard part of the talk.

"Is dinner ready, Hawkins?" Brother Tutt asked curtly.

"Yes sir."

At that moment the men started filing from the chapel, looking perked up over the prospect of food. Hawkins motioned them to follow him.

The speaker of the morning, a young jerk from some country church, emerged from the chapel, Bible in one hand, loosening his collar with the other.

"Ah Lordy, Brother Holyfield," he piped. "They've heard it one more time. Now they can take it or leave it; it's no skin off my back either way."

The troubled look on Brother Tutt's face turned to a scowl, but he smiled a cheerless smile. "Yeah... well... do go in and have dinner with the men, Brother Cork," he said hurriedly.

"No thank you," Cork turned down the invitation flatly. "I've had enough of those bums today!" He hurried off.

I thought I caught a look of downright dislike on Brother Tutt's face as he watched Cork go. Then he spoke to Jake.

"Mr. Raven," he said. "You know the rule here; you attend the services in the chapel or you don't eat." Jake bowed up to speak, but Brother Tutt cut him off. "However, I'll make an exception today since you seem to have run into some trouble." Turning to me he said, "Get him a pair of britches from the clothing room, Sam, and you two go eat."

Jake stood looking sour while I rummaged around looking for some britches.

"Looka here, Jake Raven," I said shortly. "Are you teed off 'cause Brother Tutt says you gotta listen to the preacher or you don't eat?"

"Well, he can't ram religion down my throat!"

"Nope, sure can't, so what's your beef? It's little enough for you men to do for him in exchange for his kindness to all of you."

Jake chirked up. "Right on Bro' Sam!" he joshed. "Gimme them britches, and let's go sample Bro' Hawkins' victuals before the others sample 'em up!"

Jake Raven had turned up at The Fish's Belly a month ago, hungry, ragged, and full of foolishness. Any questions we'd ever put to him were either ignored, evaded, or answered with some exaggerated jest. Once I'd caught him gazing at a child's picture on a magazine cover with his naked soul showing, but he came to himself and snapped out of it in a flash.

Once he told an inquisitive fellow at the table that his granddaddy died in the Spanish American War, and when the fellow asked how he was killed, Jake replied, deadpan, "He choked to death on peanut butter."

Jake was thin, looked as if he'd been pressed between two cement slabs, with a long face and big ears that stood away from his head. He moved quickly, drawled his words, and like I said, was forever joshing. You couldn't help liking him.

When we got to the kitchen we sat down and helped our plates. After a few bites Jake said, "Hawkins, this is the best cabbage I ever tasted. How come you to be such a good cook, anyway?"

"I learned how to cook when my wife left me," Hawkins replied.

"My wife left me," Jake said. "Claimed I was trying to kill her with a chain saw."

"A chain saw!"

"Yeah, she thought I had one in the bed with me. She mistook my snoring for a chain saw...." He started breaking up with laughter.

"So you had a wife, eh?" Hawkins observed.

Jake clammed up. He might have been a block of wood, except for his eating. Looks went around the table, but we pressed him no more.

Brother Tutt came in. Hawkins got him a plate and took up some hot victuals. Several of the men looked skittish, but that was uncalled for. It wasn't in Brother Tutt to willfully embarrass or humiliate a man who was down. He could be firm, he could be stern, but never unkind.

He had run the downtown rescue mission ever since it was started (in fact he had named it), and most people called it his, but there were others involved. I had first worked for him on his farm and then he hired me to help at the mission as it grew. Hawkins, the cook, was the only other hired help he had. The men who came and went helped out when needed.

"Sam," Brother Tutt said to me there at the table. "I want you and Jake to take the pickup truck and go out to the farm for a load of vegetables. Minnie and the kids are going to have them gathered up for us."

"Is it O.K. if I drive?" Jake spoke up. "I got my driver's license, you know. You saw it."

"Tutt, tutt, Jake," Brother Tutt said, frowning, laying an index finger along his nose. "I'd rather you let Sam drive this time. That truck has seen its best days."

"That's just it," Jake said. "That truck needs the soot blown out of it. Slow driving will clog one up."

Brother Tutt shook his head. "No Jake," he said. "I want Sam to drive."

Jake had been wanting to drive that pickup ever since he came to The Fish's Belly, insisting that it needed the soot blown out of it. But Brother Tutt had held out against it as kindly as possible.

When we got out to the farm, we found the vegetables, along with watermelons and peaches, already gathered, like Brother Tutt said. Mrs. Holyfield and the kids helped us load them, and we headed back.

About the time we got them unloaded at the mission, Brother Tutt thought of the marked-down bread special at one of the supermarkets close by. He pulled himself up, took a deep breath and turned to Jake. "You want to take the truck and go for the bread?" he asked.

Did he! Jake jumped into the old truck and maneuvered it smoothly out of the back entrance parking space and into the street. At the traffic light he turned left and headed up the avenue. As we watched, the vehicle picked up speed, and it was already popping before it was out of sight.

A troubled look moved onto Brother Tutt's face. "Tutt, tutt," he scolded, "I never should have let him do it! I'd better call Dade." Dade was a police friend of Brother Tutt's whom he knew was just going on street duty.

It was only a matter of minutes before we heard Jake coming back. He had circled the block making right turns and he roared past The Fish's Belly going south on the street, popping like a machine gun. We barely glimpsed his grinning face. I never dreamed a machine could be made to backfire like that. There were several bony dogs in his wake, yowling as if in pursuit of a deadly enemy.

Brother Tutt ran to his old car and slid under the wheel. "Come on!" was all he said, so as many of us as could loaded on. We moved into the street and took after Jake.

Two blocks later Officer Dade passed us, his siren shrieking. At First Avenue North, Dade turned left, heading east. We lost sight of him, but we followed his sound. Brother Tutt crouched over the steering wheel of his car going, "Tutt, tutt, tutt," without ceasing. He said it like a prayer. Once he broke off to say, "And the man's a rebel!"

A fire truck passed us. Dade must have radioed for it. We met the dogs with their tongues hanging out and their tails dragging.

Suddenly Hawkins shouted, "There they are!"

Brother Tutt swerved into a big parking lot on our right. The pickup truck was in the lot turned upside down.

"Lord have mercy!" I yelled. "Jake is still in that truck!"

"It's apt to catch on fire any minute," Dade told us as we unloaded.

Everybody was in action. Brother Tutt knelt on one knee beside the driver's side of the truck and hollered, "Jake, do you hear me?"

"Yes, sir," Jake answered clearly from the inside.

"Do you mind if I ram some religion down your throat?" Brother Tutt asked loudly but most politely.

"No, sir!"

Brother Tutt had to move then so the men could work. We managed to pull Jake out of the truck minutes before it caught on fire. That man laughed and laughed. Two more fire trucks pulled into the parking lot. Jake laughed a little more. In the confusion he slipped away. The last time I noticed him he was standing beside Hawkins. When I looked again he was gone. We never saw him again.

However, four months later, Brother Tutt did get a letter from Jake. Upon opening the letter he found a five dollar bill and a note. "Dear Brother Tutt, I'm awfully sorry about the truck. Here is five dollars I earned picking off potato bugs for a farmer. I hope you can use it to help pay for another truck. Jake."

The Rooster Cooker

We had laid the crop by, and me and my brother Bernie had been helping Daddy rive shingles to mend some leaks in the roof of the house. It was dinnertime, and me and Bernie got to the house a little ahead of Daddy. Soon as we walked into the kitchen where Mama was dishing up the noon meal, I saw she had something on her mind, something that excited her. Then I saw the letter from my sister Clemmie Lee on the cook table.

Clemmie Lee is married and lives in the city. She's always putting Mama up to doing things she just wouldn't just do. She nearly had Mama persuaded into getting her hair cut and a permanent wave. She tried to get her started smoking, but she failed in that, too. She did talk Mama into buying a girdle, telling her how slim and girlish she'd look. Mama never wore it but once. She said it was too tight, and she didn't care about looking girlish anyway.

"Get a bucket of water, Cliff," Mama said, before I could ask her what Clemmie Lee wrote in her letter. By the time I got the water, Daddy had come in and was washing his hands, and then we sat down to eat.

Soon as we'd had the blessing and started helping our plates, Mama said, "We got a letter from Clemmie Lee." She had a sly, pleased look on her face.

"What'd she write?" Daddy asked, as he spooned fresh field peas and okra onto his plate.

"They're all tolerable," Mama said. "She's carried away with that pressure cooker she bought two weeks ago. It's just a miracle, near 'bout. Cooks okra in one minute. She said it would cook a tough old crowed-out rooster in twenty minutes, tender enough so a baby could eat it."

"Humph!" Daddy said, forking some ripe sliced tomatoes.

"All right, you'll see," Mama chirped. "She said I ought to get one on account of the stove wood it will save if for no other reason."

"How much does it cost?" Daddy asked. He hates to cut stove wood.

"$13.94."

"Are you gonna buy it?" Bernie asked.

"Ain't a damn thing to it!" Daddy said.

"I've got enough money to buy it," Mama cooed, a dreamy, faraway expression on her face. "I could go up on the bus one day, and Clemmie Lee would carry me into town to buy the cooker the next day, and I'd come home the next."

"You think you'll go this afternoon?" Daddy asked.

"Oh no," Mama replied, "I can't make it today. I'll send the boys up to James Palmer's this afternoon to see if he can take me to Mintersville tomorrow."

Mintersville is fourteen miles away. That's where we catch a bus for the city.

"Well, boys," Daddy said, "I need you to help me, but your Mama's got to get that rooster cooker. So y'all go see if you can engage James to haul her to catch that bus tomorrow, and I'll make out the best I can." He got his hat off a nail on the wall and left. You could tell how disgusted he was by the way he walked.

Mama, flitting around the kitchen, stacking up the dishes, humming "When we all get to Heaven," seemed to think she was nearly there already.

James Palmer agreed to carry Mama to Mintersville the next day, which would be Tuesday. When we got back home about the middle of the afternoon, we set in on Mama to let us go with her. She wouldn't hear of it.

"Y'all got to help your Daddy," she said. "He's not much of a cook, but y'all can make out till I get back. I want you boys to keep the dishes washed and try to keep the chickens out of the kitchen."

"You don't care if we starve to death," Bernie pouted.

"I hate washin' old dishes!" I shouted. "It ain't a boy's place to wash dishes!"

"Why, Cliff," Mama coaxed, "you and Bernie oughta be gladder'n anything for me to get this pressure cooker. Just think how much stove wood it will save you from toting."

"Huh!" Bernie snorted, "I'll bet!"

"Well, now, y'all just be patient," Mama said. "Think how good it'll be when I'm helpin' you pull fodder, or on wash day, to come in at 11:45 and cook dinner in fifteen minutes."

That made us feel a little better.

Mama got off the next day. James roared up in his old truck at 12:30, and in a few minutes they were on the road to Mintersville.

She had left us plenty cooked for supper and a whole list of instructions. Daddy never even read the instructions, and me and Bernie never paid any attention to them.

Minnie, a neighbor who lived on the hill near us, came late that afternoon to milk the cow and strain up the milk. Mama had gone herself to engage Minnie.

"Well, Minnie, I'm without a wife," Daddy said.

Minnie laughed. "She's comin' back, Mr. Gus. She sho excited bout dat pressure cooker. I spec you be proud she got it."

"Humph," Daddy grunted. "You reckon I might get Lena Hornbuckle to marry me in case Pearl don't come back?"

Minnie tied a clean white cloth over the pitcher of milk she'd strained and set it in the refrigerator. She rolled her eyes, but she didn't laugh. "You sho is a sight, Mr. Crabtree," she said.

Daddy made biscuits the first morning Mama was gone. They were big as saucers and hard as rocks, and there was dough and flour all over the cook table as well as some on the floor.

He said let the dishes alone, and we left to help him rive shingles. At dinnertime we ate a pound of cold wieners and some stale light bread. For supper we opened a can of sauerkraut and a can of peaches.

By then Daddy wouldn't even mention Mama's name, and me and Bernie didn't mention anything. We didn't like the look on Daddy's face.

There wasn't a drop of housekeeping blood in any of us. By the second morning there was not a clean dish in the kitchen. It was easy to see the chickens hadn't been kept out. Daddy threw a big cut of butter at the wall.

"No tellin' when your Mama'll be back!" he finally said. "She'll likely get a job sellin' them damn rooster cookers!"

Minnie brought the milk in before we left to rive shingles. She took a long look at the kitchen and said, "I'm gwin clean dis kitchen up fo Mis' Pearl git back."

We were plenty glad to hear that.

At lunch we boiled a dozen eggs and ate them with sliced tomatoes and hot peppers.

About 2 p.m. Daddy said, "Well, I believe we'll knock off for today." We all came to the house and fiddled around. Daddy hauled a wheelbarrow load of manure from the barnlot to the garden. Bernie and me cleaned up where the chickens had been in the house. We were all keyed up for Mama's return with the pressure cooker.

James rattled up with her at 4:30, and she was the most pleased-looking person I ever saw in my life. We brought the big cardboard box in and set it down. Mama opened it and took the shiny pressure cooker out of its wrappings. She set it on the kitchen table and asked where Daddy was.

At that instant we heard Daddy's step on the front porch. Mama met him at the door.

"Well," she said. "I made it back."

"I didn't look for you back," Daddy said. "I was fixin' to go over and speak to Lena Hornbuckle about marrying me."

"I got the cooker. It sure is pretty. You better come see it."

They came in the kitchen.

"Yeah, that's sure pretty," Daddy said, looking at it. "Well," he added, "we ain't got but one rooster, but I guess you're gonna cook him for supper."

"Oh no," Mama said. "I thought I'd try it out on okra tonight. It says in the book you can cook okra in one minute."

"Humph!"

"That's all right," Mama said, flouncing her shoulders, "I'll show you!"

She told me and Bernie to go to the okra patch and cut a mess of okra while she changed clothes and made a fire in the stove. That made us mad as blitzy, but we was wanting to see that pressure cooker perform, so we got a bucket and some knives and took off.

By the time we got back with the okra, Mama had a fire built and a pan of cornbread in the oven.

"I'll go milk the cow," she said. "Watch the bread and put in more wood. It won't take but one minute to cook the okra after I'm through milking."

The cornbread was done when Mama came back from the cowpen. She quickly strained the milk. Then she washed and trimmed the okra and put it in the pressure cooker, sealed the lid, and set it on the stove.

We gathered around. Daddy was hoeing his marigolds in the backyard, but I could see him out the door, and he was keeping a close watch on the kitchen.

Mama had her instruction book, reading it. "First the steam has to start coming out. Then you put the gauge on and let it rise to the third notch, and it only has to cook one minute."

She put in three sticks of wood and some rich pine splinters. Turning the cornbread out onto a plate, she set it in the warming closet.

The clock on the kitchen cabinet said 6 o'clock. Our usual suppertime was 5:30.

Daddy came into the kitchen. He washed his hands and dried them carefully.

Mama fired the stove again. She wiped the sweat off her face with her apron and told me to go get some more stove wood.

"Thought you said it was gonna save stove wood!" Bernie blazed out.

"It is!" Mama said with a pinch of aggravation in her voice. "But we've got to get the pressure up. Why don't y'all just sit down now and be a little patient."

"Humph!" Daddy jeered as he whirled around and got his hat and left the house.

"Well," Mama flounced her shoulders again. "It's a pity people can't have a little more patience!"

I got the wood and flung it in the wood box. "I'm hungry!" I said. "It's 6:30!"

"Well, the pressure's up now," Mama said, sticking more wood in the stove. "So I'll put the gauge on, and when it rises to the third notch, it won't take but one minute for that okra to cook."

"You jest wasted the money you spent for that thing!" Bernie blazed out again. "You could cook okra quicker the way you been cookin' it!"

"You shore could!" I joined in, wiping my face. That kitchen was the hottest place I ever saw. All at once the gauge began to spew and jiggle.

"Let's all get back now!" Mama warned sharply. "Clemmie Lee said she heard that one blew up!"

Me and Bernie jumped back to the door. The noise on the stove was getting worse, and it sounded like a real threat to our lives. Mama stood well away from the red-hot stove, wiping her face with her apron, looking worried.

"It's gonna blow up and kill us!" I hollered. "What'd you buy it for?"

"Yeah, what'd you buy it for?" Bernie yelled. "Goin' off and leavin' us by ourselves jest to buy an old thing to kill us all!"

In a flash Mama flew mad. You let an easygoing person like her get mad, and it's awful. She switched around quick as a flea could hop and grabbed me and Bernie by our overall galluses, and she shook us like she was sifting meal with us.

"Jemminetti boys!" she squealed. "If y'all say another word about that pressure cooker, I'll blister you from one end to the other, and you neen to think I won't!"

We are usually bad to talk back to Mama, especially if Daddy's not around, but that was one time we laid low. It scared us to see Mama like that nearly as much as if we'd met a grizzly bear.

The gauge finally did come up to the third notch, and in exactly one minute Mama set the pressure cooker off the stove. It was 7:15 by the clock. The katydids were in full concert outside.

While we waited for the pressure to go down so Mama could open the cooker, Bernie and me sat at the table sulking.

After ten minutes Mama tested the cooker by lifting the gauge a tad. No steam spewed out. Mama took the lid off and dished up the okra.

"Wonder where Daddy is?" she asked cheerfully as she set the bowl on the table.

No answer.

"You reckon he's gone over to Uncle Mack's to spend the night?"

"I guess so," Bernie said. "He couldn't get nothin' to eat here!"

Mama didn't seem to even hear what he said. She took some okra on her plate with a blissful dreamlike expression on her face.

Switch-Off Gal

"Maw'nin, Mr. John." Maggie, with Lick-the-Pot, a bony hound, at her heels, came bareheaded out of the June sunshine into the cool pottery shop. "How is you dis maw'nin?"

"Good morning, Maggie. I'm all right. How are you?" Mr. John was putting handles on a plank full of half-dry churns.

"Des tolerable, Mr. John, des tolerable." Her voice took on a tone that was a cross between a wheedle and resignation. "Zedric done sont me down heah to see iffen you'd buy dem chickens an dat pig he got."

Mr. John got himself a chew of tobacco and gave Maggie a chew. "Zedric selling out?" he asked.

Maggie sighed. "Zedric done gone crazy. Dat gal up to Burninham done writ a letter an she say she comin' on a visit iffen Zedric send her ten dollars to come on." Maggie eased herself down onto an upturned churn. "Zedric ain't got no $10, so he say he gwi sell dem chickens an dat pig to git it."

Kezie Body swung through the shop door with an armload of freshly ground clay. He and Maggie exchanged greetings. Depositing the clay in a big box Kezie asked politely, "Whut yo folkses doin' Mis' Maggie?"

"Dey eatin' plums, Kezie. Eatin' plums an knockin' flies. Artolia she washin'."

"Why doesn't Zedric take his chickens and pig to the store and sell them?" Mr. John asked.

"Huh," Maggie grunted. "Zedric owe Mr. Bob. He ain't gwine 'round him wid nothin' to sell."

"He could work for me and make the money if he wasn't so infernally lazy."

"Yas suh, sho could. Dat Zedric he sho lazy."

"How many chickens does he have?"

"He got six, countin' his rooster."

"How big is his pig?"

"I'm gwi tell you de truf, Mr. John, dat pig ain' gwi weigh a bit mor'n fifty pounds on foot. Plums ain' gwi fatten no hog."

"Well, I'll give him ten dollars for 'em and not a penny more."

"Yas suh, dat's all he wants."

Maggie left. Mr. John and Kezie started carrying pottery out into the sunshine to dry. "Zedric's gal is coming down to see him," Mr. John chuckled.

"Ya suh, I hyard whu Mis' Maggie say." Kezie laughed shortly, "Hit's 'bout time," he said. "Zedric he done been braggin' 'bout his Burninham gal ever since he went up dar on dat visit las' winter."

"I guess he thinks she is going to marry him."

"Ya suh, yas suh! Dat's what he thinks. Las' Sunday he wuz struttin' roun' down at de chu'ch in dem tight faded britches braggin' 'bout Mis' Mae Anna. He say he gwi show us folkses somethin'."

"When he gets her down here you might beat his time."

Kezie looked at Mr. John. Not a muscle moved except his eyes and they were blinking erratically. Then suddenly, as if galvanized by electricity, he tore out around the drying churns like a dog with a running fit. Making a complete circle he flopped onto the ground and flounced about, laughing gustily. Then he sat up and said solemnly, "Mr. John, you sho is a sight."

"You could have some fun out of Zedric and get you a gal to boot," Mr. John said.

"Naw suh!" Kezie shook his head. "Naw suh! I ain't gwi git mixed up wid one dem city gals. Dey ain't no count fo nothin' but switch-off gals. I sho woun' mare one dem."

"Oh, you wouldn't have to marry her."

Mis' Hattie called dinner. After they had eaten, Kezie said he believed he'd go up to Maggie's house while Mr. John was resting. When he came back, Mr. John asked how things were going on the hill.

"Zedric ketchin' dem chickens," Kezie said. "Mis' Maggie she say wait an ketch 'em on de roost tonight, but Zedric he yell and say he gwi ketch 'em now. He got Cootchie, June Bug, an 'Possum atter dem chickens an dem chickens is a runnin' an a squakin'. Zedric he jumpin' an a wavin' his arms to head dem chickens off when dey starts unner de house. He so hot he shinin' lak a black diamond."

"What was Maggie doing?"

Kezie laughed. "She settin' on de piazza, dippin' dat black gum brush in dat snuff box an sayin' 'Don't you ketch non ub my chickens. I'll bust yo skull eben if you is my son!'" After a minute Kezie added, "Artolia, she churnin."

"Artolia's the only one of Maggie's children that's worth a damn," Mr. John said.

About mid-afternoon Kezie was busy splitting wood to fire the kiln while Mr. John mixed a tub of glazing when up stepped Cootchie, June Bug, and 'Possum, Maggie's grandkids, each with a wilted-looking chicken under both arms.

"Us brung dem chickens," Cootchie said.

"Pa say he ketch de pig tonight," 'Possum added. He and June Bug were Zedric's offspring from a past marriage.

"Well, put 'em in the hen house and give 'em some fresh water," Mr. John instructed.

The sun sank away in the west and Kezie went home. Now Mr. John, waiting for Mis' Hattie to strain up her milk and finish supper, was resting on the front porch. Presently he saw Maggie strolling out the road, hands crossed behind her back.

"This breeze feels fine doesn't it," Mr. John remarked as Maggie came into the yard.

"Yas suh."

"Zedric caught his chickens."

"Yas suh." She sat down on the steps. A katydid began his chant in the chinaberry tree. From over in the woods came the cry of a whippoorwill.

Maggie sighed. "I'm gwi tell you de truf, Mr. John. I had to git away frum dat house. Zedric he been writin' dat letter to dat gal evah since he got dem chickens caught. He done runned outen tobacco, an he had dem chillern runnin' to de spring atter water, an he ain't yit got dat letter writ!"

"Zedric hasn't been this romantic since Early left him, has he?"

"Naw suh. Zedric done gone wile o'er dat gal! He say he gwi show dese folkses roun' heah somethin'. Huh! Zedric do what he oughta do he put dat ten dollars in my han' to buy bread wid!"

"How is Zedric's corn crop?" Mr. John asked.

"Dat's 'nother thing," Maggie picked up the thread of vexation again. "Zedric done laid roun' an let de grass take dat cawn crop. Now he say dem chillern got to hoe it out fo dat gal come. Huh! Zedric des wanta show out. Dat cawn ain't gwi make nothin' now nohow."

"Maybe this gal could make something out of Zedric," Mr. John suggested.

Maggie rolled her eyes until only the whites showed in the gathering darkness. "Zedric thirty-two years old, Mr. John. Ain't nobody gwi make nothin' outen Zedric. Naw suh! He mare dat gal hit ain't gwi mean nothin' but 'nother passel of young'uns fo me to raise." Maggie sighed again heavily. "Dat Zonella done gone off up de country and lef Cootchie on me." Maggie indulged in a flurry of sighs and then broke out crossly, "My chillern sho do make me tired!"

"Artolia has never given you any trouble, Maggie," Mr. John pointed out.

"Naw suh. Dat's de gospel truf. Artolia she work an she ain't tryin' to meet no man at de end of ever row. She gwi make some man a wife."

The next day, which was Tuesday, Mr. John glazed, with Kezie helping. They worked steadily, Mr. John dipping the churns, jugs, pots, and bowls into the tub of glazing, setting them down, Kezie wiping the rims clean with a sponge he kept constantly washing out in a jar of water. Two pieces of pottery stacked rim to rim and then fired would bond together, so that only breaking could ever separate them if the glazing were not wiped off. As the two men worked they talked and joked about Zedric's consuming romance, and speculated on its outcome.

Wednesday they set the kiln, and Thursday Mr. John fired it. Kezie split more rich pine wood, keeping it piled handy for Mr. John to bring the kiln from a small blaze to a white-hot inferno and turn the raw pottery into stoneware, over a period of sixteen hours. There was scant opportunity for talk of any kind on firing day.

When Mr. John had drawn out his trial pieces and was satisfied there'd been sufficient firing, they mixed a mortar of mud and sealed the kiln using bricks kept for that purpose. After two days Mr. John would break the seal ever so slightly to let in a little air. Too much air at that point could cool-crack the whole kiln of pottery in a flash.

On Friday morning Mr. John was back at his wheel turning flower-pots, with Kezie making balls for him when Zedric came stepping in.

After greetings were exchanged Mr. John asked, "Have you heard from your gal, Zedric?"

"Yas suh." Zedric patted a letter in his shirt pocket. "Hit come dis while ago. She say she gwi be heah tomorrow on de bus. Is you gwine to town tomorrow, Mr. John?"

Mr. John slapped a ball of clay onto the wheel and leaned to it. "I guess I'll go," he said. "I've got some glazing at the express office and I need a new shovel."

"Whut time you gwine? Miss Mae Anna say she comin' on de ten o'clock bus."

"I guess we'll be there by ten." Mr. John laughed.

Having settled that matter Zedric turned to Kezie to ask with an air of great superiority, "How is yo crop, Kezie?"

"Hit's fine, Zedric, fine! I's 'bout ready to lay dat crop by. Den I's gwi spen all my time workin' fo Mr. John an I's gwi sho nuff git rich." He patted his hip pocket.

Setting one flat bare foot up on a block of kiln wood, Zedric stood looking at Kezie. After a long moment he asked with fine scorn, "You ain't got no gal is you, Kezie?"

"I sho ain't," Kezie said slowly, "but I mout git me one fo long." He stood still as a post, his eyes blinking. Then bang! He was gone like a dog with a fit, out the door and around the shop. Coming back inside he flopped down onto the dirt floor and lay kicking, laughing wildly.

Zedric stood looking at Kezie quizzically. Turning to Mr. John he said, "Dat Kezie need a dose of liver medicine."

It was late afternoon of the same day when Maggie came down again. Mr. John and Mis' Hattie were snapping beans to can.

"Mis' Hattie, kin yo let me hab a dozen eggs till dat 'lottment check come?" Maggie said. "Zedric he ain't gwi hush his mouf til I cooks a poun' cake fo dat gal."

"You need another boy in the service don't you, Maggie?" Mis' Hattie said.

"Sho do," Maggie agreed. "Dat Zedric he atter me fo dat money day an night. I'm gwi tell you de truf, he done des 'bout runned me crazy dis week. He ain't missed a day pressin' dem britches and dat yellow tie he got. He been rubbin dem shoes wid my grease an he got 'em settin' under de bed wid a sack spread o'er dem."

"Did they get the corn hoed out?" Mr. John asked, taking a chew of tobacco and giving Maggie a chew.

"Dey don't lak much," Maggie said. "Zedric he done hollered til he hoarse. He had 'em sweepin' dem yards til dey ain't no dirt lef, an we's 'bout choked to def wid dat dust." She spit and snorted.

Mis' Hattie got the eggs for Maggie, who sighed. "Mis' Hattie kin yo l'emme hab a smidgen of vanilla? Zedric done took dat I had to go on his head tomorrow."

By a little after sunup Saturday morning Zedric was seated in Mr. John's truck. About the time Mr. John came out, Kezie walked up with preacher Lee Rutledge. Kezie was dressed in his Sunday best.

"Is you gwine to town, Kezie?" Zedric asked.

"I'm ain't gwine to war," Kezie replied.

The bus from Birmingham was arriving as Mr. John parked his truck by the courthouse square. Zedric leaped out running.

"Zedric look lak a 'lectrified ant," Kezie said.

"You better not take a laughing fit now, Kezie," Mr. John warned sharply. "You'll get put in jail."

"Mr. Zedric say he gwi hab a job fo me today or tomorrow," Preacher Lee said soberly.

"Hot dawg!" Kezie hollered. His eyes were bulging like cork stoppers. Mae Anna was getting off the bus.

"She's bright as glory, isn't she?" Mr. John said as Mae Anna, in a brilliant green dress of crepe georgette and a wide brimmed screaming-yellow hat, descended into Zedric's arms.

Throwing back his shoulders, tilting his hat cockily, Kezie stepped out ahead of Mr. John and Preacher Lee, heading for the bus.

"He's going to try to beat Zedric's time," Mr. John said.

"We is sholy goin' to hab trubble," Preacher Lee predicted.

"Po little ole me needs a cigareet," Mae Anne was shrilling as Mr. John and Preacher Lee walked up.

Pulling out his tobacco and papers Zedric began frantically making a cigarette.

"Hab one on me, Miss Mae Anna." Kezie stepped up to offer her one from his pack of ready rolls.

"Who is you?" Mae Anna fluttered.

"Dat Kezie Body!" Zedric snapped. "Come on Sugah Lump, us got to buy some stuff." Taking her firmly by the arm, he led her away.

After supper that night, Mr. John said he believed he'd mosey off up to Maggie's and see what was going on. Walking through the heavily dewed grass, smelling the sweet wild honeysuckle, he reflected that it was no wonder Kezie and Zedric were stirred up romantically. Starting to climb the hill he heard footsteps and turning, he discerned Kezie with his banjo.

"Hello, Kezie, you going up to Maggie's?"

"Yas suh." He shifted his banjo. "Can't stay 'way, Mr. John. Dat gal done put her stingaree on me."

"You think you can beat Zedric's time?"

"I done beat it. Zedric don't know it but I is. I showed Miss Mae Anna my money today in town an I done beat dat Zedric's time."

"You thinking about marrying her?"

Kezie was silent. "Mr. John," he said finally, "I'se all churned up on de inside. I don't know what I'se gwi do. Dat gal ain't nothin' but a switch-off gal, but she done put her stingaree on me."

They walked on and presently Kezie began to gurgle with laughter. "Artolia done tole me somethin' funny," he said. "She down in de field today when Zedric brung Miss Mae Anna by to see his cawn. Miss Mae Anna she say, 'How come it so sho't and yellar?'" Kezie threw down his banjo and started stomping one foot and clapping his hands. When he stopped he said soberly, "Zedric he say 'Hit's des dat kinda cawn. Hit's gwi make a hunnert bushels to de acre.'"

Lick-the-Pot barked as they came into Maggie's yard. "Dat you, Mr. John?" Maggie queried.

"Yes. It's me and Kezie."

A chair hitched at the far end of the porch. "Hello dar, Mr. Kezie," Mae Anna exclaimed. "Is you got yo banjo?"

"I sho is."

"Come on o'er wid Zedric and me an play po little ole me a tune."

Sitting down on the edge of the porch, Kezie leaned against a post and began to play and sing.

"Stacker Lee Lee
Don't be so bad.
Think about de trubble
Dat I've done had!
Stacker—oh Stacker Lee."

At the other end of the porch, Mr. John got himself a chew of tobacco and gave Maggie a chew. In the moonlight he could make out the forms of the little children sitting about on the floor. Artolia, her chair tilted against the wall, sat a bit apart from the rest.

"Dat gal ain't no 'count, Mr. John," Maggie leaned close to say while Kezie played. "She done got Zedric riled up. She makin' eyes at Kezie. Zedric done had dat whetstone rubbin' dat knife he got."

Kezie finished his tune. "Hoo-ray fo Mr. Kezie!" Mae Anna applauded. "Can you play, Zedric?"

"Naw!"

"You's a slow leak, ain't you big boy? Is you got a cigareet, Mr. Kezie? Zedric's all gone. He des had nuff money to buy one pack. Hit sho do take lots of cigareets fo po little ole me."

Zedric leaped up, turning his chair over on his way to the water bucket, where he made a loud clatterment with the dipper as he got himself a drink.

"Zedric gwi catch on fiah," Artolia said dryly. The children sniggered.

"Shut up!" Zedric hollered. Old Lick-the-Pot shot off the porch, bumping his bones as he went under the house.

"You gwi scare po little ole me to def," Mae Anna whimpered.

"Hit's bedtime," Zedric announced sullenly.

But when Mr. John left, Kezie was still playing his banjo though the moon had climbed high in the cloudless summer night sky.

Mr. John was piddling around his shop Sunday morning when Kezie came stepping in, wet with sweat. Mr. John saw right away that he had something on his mind.

"How did you make out last night, Kezie?" Mr. John asked.

"Awl right." He walked around kicking up dust on the dirt floor. Taking out a big red handkerchief, he mopped his face and neck. Finally he spoke. "Mr. John, I'se gwi mare dat gal."

"Have you asked her?"

"Naw suh. Dat Zedric he stickin' to her lak a tick but she gwi mare me. Dat gal done put her stingaree on me an my mine is made up. I'se gwi show her dis." He pulled a roll of money out of his pocket.

"You worked hard for that money, Kezie."

"Yas suh. He stood looking down at the dirt floor a short while, then raising his head he said, "I'se gwine up to Mis' Maggie's."

Sunday dinner was over. Mis' Hattie, having cleaned up her kitchen, was resting on the front room bed where she could catch any breeze that might stir. Curiosity made Mr. John restless so he walked off up to Maggie's. He found her sitting alone on the cool side of the house, dipping snuff.

"Evenin' Mr. John. Have a seat."

Mr. John sat down. "Where is everybody?"

"Dey gone to see Kezie's cawn."

Mr. John laughed.

"Hit ain't funny, Mr. John. We's gwi hab trubble. Zedric he mad as a singed yellar jacket. Dat Kezie he struttin'. He call hisself beatin'

Zedric's time. Zedric an Kezie bof actin' lak fools. All dat gal atter is gettin' whut dey got an she gwi be gone frum heah!" Maggie wiped the sweat from her face with her apron.

"Did Zedric get her to church this morning?"

"Naw suh!" Maggie spit. "Mr. John, dat gal ain't studyin' 'bout chu'ch bit mo'n old Lick-de-Pot." After a brief silence Maggie said, "Brudder Lee he comed to see 'bout dem atter chu'ch an he et dinner wid us."

"Lee knew you'd have chicken. Is he gone with them to see Kezie's corn?"

"Yas suh."

They sat silent, watching an old speckled hen and her half-naked chicks wallowing in the dust under a rose bush.

Suddenly Maggie spoke. "Whut dat?"

A keen wail of distress came from up the hill the way the road ran.

"Dat Zedric!" Scrambling out of her chair Maggie ran swaying and moaning across the yard.

Zedric came down the hill like a bullet. "Git de kerosene! Git de kerosene!" he squealed as he sprinted through the yard and leaped up onto the porch. "I'se snake bit! I'm gwi die! I'm gwi die," he moaned, slinging off one shoe to stick his foot in the pan of kerosene Maggie had brought.

"What kind of a snake was it?" Mr. John asked.

"Hit wuz a rattlesnake! I'm gwi die. You reckon I'm gwi die?"

"Whar de res' of 'em?" Maggie asked, pouring kerosene over Zedric's foot, pressing it to make it bleed.

"Dey comin'. I lef 'em. I'm gwi' die, I'm gwi die!"

At that moment the others came in sight over the hill, pressing hard, with Preacher Lee leading, in a hullaballoo of mournful noise.

"Be still, Zedric," Mr. John said, "and let me see that bite." Grasping Zedric's foot firmly in his hand he examined it. "That's no snake bite," he said. "That's a little piece of rock stuck in your ankle."

Zedric flopped over onto the floor and lay still, breathing hard. Maggie spit.

"What happened?" Mr. John asked as the rest drew up.

"Lick-de-Pot he bay a snake," Preacher Lee panted. "Zedric he say he gwi kill dat snake."

"Dat Zedric he des wanta show out fo dat gal," Maggie muttered.

"Was this after you had seen Kezie's corn?" Mr. John asked.

"Sholy, sholy. Zedric he got him a long pole an he flewed in to beatin' dem bushes an de snake bit him."

"Whar Kezie?" Zedric sat up suddenly. He glanced all around wildly. "What Miss Mae Anna?" He sprang to his feet. "Whey dey?"

"Dey gone," Artolia said.

"Which a way dey gone?" Zedric screamed, flinging off his other shoe.

"Dey gone towa'ds de big road."

Maggie grabbed Zedric's arm. He shook her loose. "I'm gwi kill 'em," he sobbed hysterically. "I'm gwi cut 'em bof wide open!"

"You better stay here, Zedric," Mr. John warned, but Zedric was gone as fast as he could go.

"Go with him, Lee, and don't let them hurt each other," Mr. John directed.

"Sholy, sholy," and Lee took off after Zedric.

"I'se gwine too," Artolia announced, putting her long legs in motion up the hill.

"Dat Artolia, she lak dat Kezie," Maggie sighed. "Git back heah you chilluns!" she yelled as the little ones started out after Lee and Artolia.

Mr. John went on back home then and told Mis' Hattie what had happened. He said he believed he'd just let Kezie and Zedric work out their problem without any more advice from him. He felt a little troubled over encouraging Kezie to beat Zedric's time.

Kezie didn't come back to work for Mr. John until Tuesday. Speaking briefly, he started shoveling clay into the clay mill.

"When you finish filling the mill, you can make me some balls, Kezie," Mr. John said. "I think the mule will grind without anyone to drive her."

"Yas suh."

Mr. John went inside and started turning gallon jugs at the wheel. The creak of the wheel and the noise of a dirt dauber were the only sounds audible. He was cutting the fifth jug from the wheel when Kezie came in. Getting some clay from the clay box he started working it at the table. Taking the jug up with his lifters, Mr. John set it carefully onto a plank beside the others. He spit a long stream of tobacco juice onto the floor.

"How'd you come out with your courting, Kezie?" he asked.

Kezie slapped the two pieces of clay together. Turning his head sideways he rolled his eyes at Mr. John. "Dat gal done got my money an' gone," he said.

"How did she get it?"

Kezie put the clay down, turned and leaned against the table, wiping his face with both sleeves. "Us went to see my cawn," he began laboriously. "Dat gal she took on over dat cawn. Zedric he so mad he near 'bout crazy. Lick-de-Pot he bay dat snake. Zedric he 'bout to bust to show off fo dat gal so he grab a stick an' say he gwi kill dat snake. He commenced whomping an' den he let out a scream an' he took off."

Going to the shop door, Kezie threw a piece of clay at the mule to start her up again. He came back to the clay table and went on gloomily. "All de res' took off atter Zedric so I grabs dat gal's hand an I say, 'Les go,' an us went tother way. Us rested in a shade jes fo us got to de big road, an I showed her my money. Den I ax her if she gwi mare me. She coo lak a dove an she say, 'Sho,' an den she say sweet as candy, 'Kin I hole yo money?'"

Mr. John burst out laughing.

Kezie's smile was sickly. "So I let her hole it. Den she say, 'Sugah honey, I'se dying fo some water. Kin you go back to dat spring us passed an bring po little ole me a drink in dat can us saw?' She look lak she gwi faint so I went."

"And that's the last time you saw her."

"Dat's de las time I saw her." Kezie let his arms flop hopelessly at his sides.

"She caught a ride over on the big road."

"Yas suh! Dat's whut she done! I hyard a car stop jes fo I got back. I runned as fas' as I could but hut pulled off fo I dar an' she gone."

Mr. John slapped another ball of clay onto the wheel. "Well, Kezie," he said. "I hate I put you up to trying to beat Zedric's time."

"Dat's all right, Mr. John. Hit woun' made no difference iffen you had or iffen you hadn't. Dem switch-off gals dey drive folkses crazy."

"Did Zedric find you?"

"Yas suh. Him an Artolia an Brudder Lee met up wid me as I wuz comin' back. Zedric he screech an wave dat knife roun' an' kick up his heels lak a jackass an' he say he gwi cut me open."

"What did you do?"

Kezie balled his fists until his muscles rippled. "I grab him in de neck an' I say, 'Git outen my way you Zedric Dobines fo I sallivate you! Iffen you'd lef dat no count switch-off gal up to Burninham what she b'longs I'd still hab my money!'"

"'Whar Mae Anna?' he yell."

"'She gone,' I say. 'She got my money an she gone in a car.' Den Zedric he start squallin' an hollerin' 'bout dem chickens an dat pig."

"What did you do then?"

"I didn' do nothin. Artolia she took hole of my han', and us comed on home."

ORDER FORM

THE WEANING
and other stories

Nell Brasher's stories are the kind of fiction that everyone from a university scholar to a high school student will read and re-read and love for life.

Only $19.95 plus $3 shipping & handling
Ala. residents add 7% sales tax

Use this form to order by mail.

Please send me ______ books.

Ship to:

Name ______________________________

Address ______________________________

City ____________________ State ________ Zip ________

Phone (____) ______________

*Please note we cannot ship to PO boxes, so include street address if necessary. If no street address is available, please add $2 to your shipping and handling charge to ensure parcel post delivery.

Method of payment:

❑ Check enclosed ❑ Money order ❑ VISA ❑ MasterCard

Card Number ______________________________

Expiration Date ____________ Signature ____________________

Make checks payable to and mail to: CRANE HILL PUBLISHERS
2923 Crescent Avenue / Birmingham, AL 35209
(800) 841-2682 / Fax (205) 871-7337